FUN—INDIAN STYLE

Carlotta released Skye at last, and sighed with contentment. "It was wonderful. We had so much *fun*."

"Hell, Carlotta, that's what it's supposed to be, ain't it? Fun?" Skye asked.

"Oh, yes, but usually you white men—and your women, too, I am afraid—make it all such a solemn game."

"Now how would you know that?" Skye said.

"I am not an innocent, Skye," Carlotta said. Then, smiling, she looked down at his naked body and reached for him. "Now it is my turn to show you what fun can be. . . ."

Exciting Westerns by Jon Sharpe

Prices higher in Canada

THE TRAILSMAN 44

SCORPION TRAIL

by
Jon Sharpe

A SIGNET BOOK

NEW AMERICAN LIBRARY

PUBLISHER'S NOTE

This novel is a work of fiction. Names, characters, places, and incidents either are the product of the author's imagination or are used fictitiously, and any resemblance to actual persons, living or dead, events, or locales is entirely coincidental.

NAL BOOKS ARE AVAILABLE AT QUANTITY DISCOUNTS WHEN USED TO PROMOTE PRODUCTS OR SERVICES. FOR INFORMATION PLEASE WRITE TO PREMIUM MARKETING DIVISION. NEW AMERICAN LIBRARY, 1633 BROADWAY. NEW YORK. NEW YORK 10019.

This first chapter of this book previously appeared in *Mesquite Manhunt*, the forty-third volume in this series.

 SIGNET TRADEMARK REG. U.S. PAT. OFF. AND FOREIGN COUNTRIES
REGISTERED TRADEMARK—MARCA REGISTRADA
HECHO EN CHICAGO. U.S.A.

SIGNET, SIGNET CLASSIC, MENTOR, PLUME, MERIDIAN AND NAL BOOKS are published by New American Library, 1633 Broadway, New York, New York 10019

First Printing, August, 1985

1 2 3 4 5 6 7 8 9

PRINTED IN THE UNITED STATES OF AMERICA

The Trailsman

Beginnings ... they bend the tree and they mark the man. Skye Fargo was born when he was eighteen. Terror was his midwife, vengeance his first cry. Killing spawned Skye Fargo, ruthless, cold-blooded murder. Out of the acrid smoke of gunpowder still hanging in the air, he rose, cried out a promise never forgotten.

The Trailsman, they began to call him, all across the West: searcher, scout, hunter, the man who could see where others only looked, his skills for hire but not his soul, the man who lived each day to the fullest, yet trailed each tomorrow. Skye Fargo, the Trailsman, the seeker who could take the wildness of a land and the wanting of a woman and make them his own.

1861—Deep in the Superstition Mountains, where the Apache's lance and the scorpion's sting are no match for greed-crazed white men.

1

It was late afternoon of a miserably hot day when Fargo rode into the sun-bleached town of Tularo, Arizona, the broiling sun a heavy hand pushing him down onto his sweaty saddle. The Ovaro he rode had held up well so far, but the pinto's head was beginning to droop noticeably.

Fargo clopped down Tularo's hard-baked main street until he came to the town's livery, a crooked, unpainted barn with a huge pile of manure in the alley beside it. Dismounting, he led the pinto into the barn, found an empty stall, and unsaddled him. He told the stable boy to rub the Ovaro down thoroughly after watering and graining him, then tossed him a coin and left the livery. Lugging his bedroll and rifle, Fargo crossed the street and entered the Arizona House, a three-story, wooden-frame hotel that was easily the most impressive building in Tularo.

Slapping the dust off his buckskins, Fargo held up for a minute in the small lobby. Potted palms had been placed hopefully about it, a few of them visibly wilting in the stifling heat. The cuspidors were caked brown with dried tobacco juice, and the bare floor around them was stained a rich mahogany.

The desk clerk was a surprise.

She was a pretty, brown-eyed, deeply tanned young girl dressed with amazing decorum, considering the heat. Her opulent auburn curls were tied up into prim buns at the back of her head. Her long-sleeved dress was starched, her collar buttoned at the neck; and so high were her breasts that Fargo was certain she was wearing a corset. Though slightly dazed by the heat, she greeted him with a cool smile.

"A room for the night, sir?"

"Yes." Fargo signed the register. As the girl handed him his key, he smiled at her and said, "I sure would like to scrub some of this dust off, ma'am, but I didn't see a barbershop when I rode in. You got any idea where the closest tubs are?"

"In the back room," she said. "On each floor. I'll heat the water and bring it up." A mischievous smile flickered for a moment on her pretty face. "You'd be surprised how seldom we get calls for bath water in this godforsaken place."

"I guess I would be, at that."

"Give me a few minutes, please."

"Of course. And thank you." Starting for the stairs, he paused and looked back at the girl. "I don't have a robe."

"I'll bring one."

Fargo thanked her and headed for the stairs.

* * *

The girl was waiting for him in the back room, the place dim with steam. She was still dressed in her high-necked dress, and Fargo caught a glimpse of the tips of her patent-leather, high-button shoes peeking out from under her long woolen skirt. A large, high-backed iron tub was sitting in the center of the room, already half-filled with hot water, and on the floor beside the waiting girl were four steaming buckets. The robe she had promised him was hanging on a hook beside the door.

He closed the door behind him.

"Undress," she said, "and give me your clothes. I'll wash them and have them back dry by morning. The sun will see to that."

The girl made no effort to look away as Fargo pulled off his boots and socks and shrugged out of his sweat-heavy buckskins and underdrawers, nor did she comment or change her expression as she watched him stride, stark-naked, over to the tub and step gingerly into the steaming water.

Fargo almost yanked his foot back out with a howl. Instead, he kept it in, sweat streaming down his forehead, then eased in all the way, his lean, powerfully muscled body adjusting gradually as he lowered himself silently into the near-scalding water. He felt as if he were plunging into the first ring of the Inferno, but made no comment as the girl, her sleeves rolled up and her dress now unbuttoned at the neck, lathered his face swiftly and proceeded to shave him. She worked swiftly and deftly, and when she had finished, she emptied one of the buckets of steaming water over his head and shoulders.

This time, he was certain she had scalded him to

death. He grabbed the sides of the tub to prevent himself from leaping out of it. When his body finally adjusted, he opened his eyes to find the girl's face leaning close to his, the faintest suggestion of a smile on her puckish mouth as she worked with a bar of yellow soap and sponge, scrubbing the dirt on his shoulders, arms, and chest. He began to relax, relishing each stroke of her sponge. His pores streamed perspiration and the suds filled the tub as he leaned back and closed his eyes, almost falling asleep as she methodically laved his body.

Abruptly, she began soaping his thick, jet-black hair. Stinging suds flowed down his forehead into the corners of his eyes. He grimaced as the girl's strong fingers began massaging his scalp. Without warning, she shoved his head forward into the steaming, foamy water. He tried to straighten up, but she pushed his head down farther, keeping him under for a moment longer, then allowed him to straighten up. As he did so, blowing like a seal, another bucket of scalding water cascaded down over him.

He gasped and fought for breath as the steam enveloped him, but she paid no heed to his discomfort and began to scrub down his back with a hard-bristle brush. Once he had gained his breath, he relaxed as he felt the miles of sand and dirt peeling off him. And the girl made no effort to hide her pleasure while she contemplated Fargo's heavily muscled torso and massive shoulders as she scrubbed over them and then down the front of him, moving for the first time well past the thick mat of short, curly hair on his chest.

As the girl scrubbed away, her fresh, round face came close to Fargo's. She smiled openly at him then, her teeth flashing brilliantly in her tanned face as her hand no longer shied away from what it found between his legs. As her swift fingers worked down into Fargo's crotch, they destroyed what little composure he had left.

She pulled way then and stood up. With the back of her hand she brushed a stray lock of hair off her damp forehead.

"Stand up," she told him, her dark eyes flashing.

Reluctantly, Fargo pushed himself to his full height. The girl did not embarrass him by commenting with word or glance on his involuntary erection. Ignoring it altogether, she busied herself in scrubbing down the small of his back, his buttocks, and the back of his legs. She was very thorough. Fargo could feel still more miles of dust peeling off, and maybe this time a good pound of skin with it.

Two more steaming buckets of hot water rinsed him, and then the girl folded a huge towel about his torso and helped him to step out of the tub. She patted him dry then, her hands playing a maddening tune over his suddenly alive body. She draped another towel over his dripping head and he rubbed his hair dry with it. He heard the door close.

She was gone.

Dressed in fresh buckskins and feeling at least five pounds lighter, Fargo left the hotel and walked down the street to the sheriff's office. The deputy, a lanky, reptilianlike creature was sitting on the jailhouse porch, his chair tipped back, his long legs braced against the railing. Thumbing his hat brim off his face, he told

Fargo that Sheriff Hammond was at the restaurant, eating his supper.

Fargo thanked the deputy and kept going until he came to Stella's Eats and entered. Stella was a large blonde piloting her course through the crush of tables as lightly as a gas-filled balloon. Despite the heat and the dark patches of sweat running down from under her enormous arms, she remained determinedly cheerful as she pointed out to Fargo the sheriff's table.

Hammond was eating alone, with a single-minded intensity that explained fully the flab larding his shoulders and the pasty, hanging jowls that gave his face a downcast look. His mouth full, he gestured with his fork toward a chair and continued to assault the mashed potatoes and gravy on his plate. A well-gnawed T-bone sat in a congealed red puddle alongside the potatoes. Thick slabs of buttered homemade white bread sat on a saucer beside his coffee. Hammond finished chewing the load of potatoes he had just delivered to his mouth and glared at Fargo.

"What's so important, mister?" he demanded. "Can't your business wait till I finish my supper?"

Fargo smiled easily, determined not to take offense. He was still feeling the effects of his marvelous bath. "Sorry to bother you, Hammond. But this won't take long."

The sheriff put down his fork. Grabbing a slice of bread, he began mopping up the remains of his mashed potatoes. "Well, see that it don't."

"I understand a shipment of silver was sent through the Superstition Mountains a couple months ago and got held up or lost. That right?"

Hammond nodded, his piggish eyes narrowing. "If you know so much, why you got to bother me?"

Fargo leaned back and smiled. This smile was not easy. "I'm looking for a man said to be involved. He went with the mule team, but his body wasn't found with the others."

"Federico Silva."

"Was that his name?"

"Your hearin' all right, is it?"

"Did you know him?"

The sheriff shrugged. "Saw him a coupla times, I guess. Never noticed nothin' about him."

Fargo described the man he was looking for and asked the sheriff if he recognized him as Silva. The sheriff downed the bread and potatoes and gravy in one huge gulp, then reached for another slice of bread. "I told you. I never noticed nothin' special about Silva. Silva could be your man, I suppose, but I wouldn't want to swear on it." The sheriff mopped up the remains on his plate and shoved them into his mouth as dark fingers of gravy dribbled over the rough stubble on his chin.

"You got any idea who attacked the train?" Fargo asked.

"Sure. Apaches or Papagos. Take your pick."

"Did you go after the Apaches to see if they got the silver?"

"You out of your head? That's Apache country, and them devils ain't half so bad as the scorpions. I'd sooner march into the bowels of hell as go after them Apaches. We found what was left of the wagons, buried the bodies we found, and pulled our asses back out of there. Them damn fools should never've tried to take that shortcut through the Superstitions." He reached for a thick wedge of apple pie. "Now let me eat."

"Thank you, Sheriff," Fargo said, pushing his chair back and standing up.

Hammond's hand was reaching for his fork. For a second or two Fargo debated whether or not to shove the lawman's face down into the pie. Then with a weary shrug, he skirted the table and left the restaurant. Although he was hungry enough when he entered the place, his interview with the sheriff had ruined his appetite.

He crossed the street to the saloon, where he purchased a bottle of bourbon and proceeded to wash the dust off his tonsils. He dined on a plate of cheese and hardtack set out on the bar, then retired to a table along one wall, waiting for his irritation with the sheriff and his frustration at finding out so little about Federico Silva to burn itself out. . . .

It was dark and Fargo was close to calling it a day when a sharp cry caused him to glance over at a corner of the saloon where a poker game was in progress.

"Grab his arm," someone cried.

One of the poker players—a thin-faced bald fellow—leapt up from the table as two other players, one on each side of him, grabbed his arms. His chair striking the floor behind him sounded like a gunshot in the small saloon.

Fargo stood up and peered over the heads of the men closing about the poker players and saw the bald man attempting to claw his way free of the two men restraining him. But they held him fast, and as Fargo watched, he saw a playing card protruding from the struggling poker player's extra-wide cuff—an ace of spades.

It stood out like a wart on a whore's cheek.

The poker player snatched his arm back and watched in a kind of dazed horror as the ace of spades fluttered to the floor. The two men holding him let go, and as the unlucky gambler slammed back against the wall, one of them—a tall, cadaverous blade of a man with a drooping, tobacco-stained mustache—reached back for his six-gun.

"Stand back, Jed," the lanky fellow told his companion. "This cheatin' son of a bitch might have a belly gun on him."

Jed took a hasty step backward and drew his own weapon.

In desperation, the gambler flung a chair at the tall one, drew a mean little derringer from his belt, and aimed it at Jed. The two men fired simultaneously. The twin detonations thundered deafeningly as thick clouds of gunsmoke obscured the men.

Through the smoke, Fargo saw Jed drop his gun and pitch forward onto the floor. The bald gambler, his face ashen, dropped his derringer and grabbed at his right shoulder. Blood streamed through his fingers.

"Jed's gut-shot!" someone cried.

The onlookers crowded closer and stared down at Jed. The doomed man was writhing in agony as blood pulsed in a black, steaming flow through his fingers. An old man knelt beside Jed, then called for a doctor. Someone near the door turned and rushed from the saloon as others, drawn by the sound of gunfire, crowded in through the batwings.

The tall man turned and glared at the wounded gambler, covering him with his Colt. The bald man, still clutching at his bleeding shoulder, took a frightened step back.

"This son of a bitch swings," the tall man told those crowding around, his voice cutting like a knife through the saloon. "Someone get a rope!"

There was a quick roar of agreement as two men dashed from the place.

"No," the gambler cried. "You've got to give me a trial. I'm a wounded man. I shot Jed in self-defense."

Harsh, contemptuous laughter greeted his plea as quick hands dragged him, still protesting, from the saloon. Fargo followed out after them and saw them heading down the street toward the livery barn.

As the tall fellow who was now in charge paused momentarily under a streetlamp, Fargo got a better look at him. There was not an ounce of extra tallow on the man, his rake-handle slimness making him appear taller than his six feet. His wrists, long and slender, hung far out of his coat sleeves, and his dark eyes sat in deep hollows. It was clear he would brook no interference—and there appeared to be no one in town prepared to go against him.

Fargo watched as Sheriff Hammond and his deputy hurried past to overtake the tall man. Pulling him around, the sheriff demanded, "What happened, John? I heard shots!"

"We finally caught Percy cheatin'," John replied. "And this time, dead to rights. The son of a bitch went for his belly gun and blasted poor Jed in the gut. Jed's back there on the floor now, bleeding to death."

Hammond swallowed. "Did Jed draw on him?"

"Damn right. And so did I."

"That means Percy shot Jed in self-defense. We got to give Percy a fair trial."

"Don't give me none of that shit," John told the sheriff. "We got a job to do, and you two ain't goin' to stop us."

Hammond appeared ready to protest, but the tall fellow placed his hand on the sheriff's shoulder and spun him out of his way and continued on after the others.

Hammond and the deputy watched him go. Then both men shrugged, apparently washing their hands of the affair, and started toward Fargo on their way back to the saloon.

Fargo blocked their progress. "Sheriff, you and this here deputy goin' to let them string that feller up?"

"What's it to you, stranger?"

"I just wanted to hear you two lawmen admit it, that's all."

"Hell," Hammond blustered, "this here lynching's only savin' the taxpayers of this town an expensive trial."

Fargo looked at both men for a long moment, then brushed contemptuously on past them after the mob. It had reached the stable by this time, and Fargo saw a rope flung up over a beam and snake its way back down to the crowd. A small fellow standing under the beam was almost finished fashioning one end of the rope into a hangman's noose, and two other men were leading a saddled horse out of the livery.

The gambler Percy—his face pale, quivering with terror—was being held upright by three men, two at his sides and one just behind him. Blood was still seeping from his shoulder wound, but no one paid any attention to it. Fargo wondered how in hell they intended to get the poor son of a bitch up onto the horse.

"Hey, Carswell," someone called to the tall man. "You goin' to do the honors?"

John Carswell nodded emphatically and spat a gob of tobacco juice onto the ground beside him. "Since it was Jed this bastard killed," he barked, "I'd consider it a pleasure!"

Everyone stepped back to allow Carswell to move closer. Percy, close to sobbing out his terror by this time, shrank back in horror as Carswell strode toward him.

"Mount up, you son of a bitch," Carswell told him.

"I can't!" Percy quavered. "I'm hurt bad!"

"That so?" inquired Carswell comically, cocking an eyebrow as he glanced around at his audience. "Well, now, you can relax, Percy. This rope's just the medicine for you. In a few minutes, I guarantee you won't feel a thing." Carswell clapped a bony claw of a hand on Percy's good shoulder and hauled him over toward the horse.

"Hold it right there!" Fargo told him, stepping between Carswell and the horse. "Maybe you better think this over, Carswell."

Carswell peered in startled surprise at Fargo. "Get the hell out of my way, stranger."

Fargo smiled coldly, but did not move. "This is

murder. I saw the whole thing. This man has a trial due him."

"Who the hell dealt you into this?" Carswell demanded furiously.

"I did," Fargo told him quietly.

With a sudden sweep of his arm, Carswell shoved Fargo violently to one side, then told the fellow who had fashioned the hangman's noose to throw it over to him. As soon as Carswell caught it, he dropped it over Percy's head and was about to boost the terrified gambler up onto the horse when Fargo rested the muzzle of his Colt against Carswell's temple.

Carswell froze.

"Now," Fargo told him quietly, "you just tell these assholes to go on home to their beds or back to the saloon."

Astounded at Fargo's action, the crowd shrank back. Carswell took a deep breath and turned his head cautiously to face Fargo, who poked the barrel up under Carswell's chin and smiled.

"You'll regret this," Carswell said, his narrow face dark with fury.

"I'd regret it a whole lot more if I stood by and let your bravos hang this here gambler. You know damn well it was self-defense. Both you men drew on him."

"All I know for sure, you big silly son of a bitch, is you better not let that four-flusher escape this rope."

"That ain't for you or me to say—only a judge and a jury."

"What's your name, mister?"

"Fargo. Skye Fargo."

"You a stranger in these parts?"

Fargo nodded. "Quit the stalling now and tell this

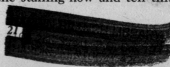

lynch mob to back off. Maybe they could go find a cat to scald."

Carswell held up a moment, his malevolent dark eyes measuring Fargo's determination. And evidently what he saw in Fargo's cold, lake-blue eyes convinced him.

"All right, boys," he called. "You heard the man. Back off."

"And give me that rope."

Carswell handed it to Fargo, who lifted it off the trembling gambler's neck and flung it away. The fellow still holding Percy released him and stepped hastily back.

The moment Percy felt himself no longer under constraint, he took complete leave of his senses. He bolted through the thinning crowd, knocking over a youngster in his haste to get away. Once in the clear, he started to race down the street with an amazing burst of speed.

"He's escapin'!" Carswell cried.

At once, six-guns thundered as a rapid volley of fire erupted from the crowd, shattering windows, springing leaks in barrels, causing horses to shy and break away in terror from the hitching racks. Not twenty yards from the stable, Percy staggered, then crumpled to the ground, his bleeding carcass jolting with each round's impact.

Slowly Fargo holstered his weapon. Carswell did the same, then turned to face Fargo.

"You better not be thinkin' of stayin' in this town, mister."

"I'll be stayin' as long as I please," Fargo said.

"Yeah? Well, the next time you draw on me, you better be prepared to pull the trigger."

Fargo tipped his head and smiled. "Hell, Carswell, what makes you think I wasn't prepared to do it this time?"

Turning, Fargo pushed his way through the crowd. He could feel Carswell's cold eyes boring into his back, but did not pause or look around as he mounted the hotel's porch and went inside.

An aged cowpoke with sad eyes and gaunt features hurried to get back around behind the front desk. It was clear the fellow had abandoned his post to watch the excitement outside. He stared at Fargo cautiously as Fargo asked him where the other desk clerk was, the girl.

"You mean Miss Poole?"

"If that's her name."

"She ain't no desk clerk." He sniffed and sent a dark stream of chewing tobacco at a cuspidor to his right. "That's Emma Poole. She's the owner."

Fargo frowned. "A young girl—all done up in starched woolen dress and patent-leather shoes?"

"You want Miss Poole should go around in pants?"

Fargo shrugged. "Sorry," he said, then asked for the key to his room.

He was suddenly very tired.

Not long after, a somewhat depleted bottle of bourbon on the floor beside him, Fargo lay on his bed staring up at a crack in the ceiling as he gloomily pondered the day's adventures.

He had not exactly covered himself with glory. His foolhardy attempt to stop the lynching had only made the sheriff and his deputy look bad and turned a stranger into an implacable foe. The moment that damn fool of a gambler got his ass blown off, the joke was on Fargo.

Fargo shook his head. Served him right for meddling. It was always a bad idea. Maybe someday he would learn. If he lived that long.

He was reaching for the bourbon when someone knocked lightly on his door. Since he didn't know anyone in this town—no one that was friendly, that is—he reached swiftly under the pillow for his Colt and swung off the bed.

The light rap came again.

On bare feet he padded across the room and flattened himself against the wall beside the door. "Who is it?"

"Me."

Fargo recognized the voice at once. Emma Poole. He turned the key in the lock and opened the door. She stepped quickly inside. Her thick, auburn hair was combed out, even though she was still wearing that high-necked, long-sleeved dress.

Fargo closed the door behind her. "What can I do for you, ma'am?"

She looked at the gun in his hand. "First, you can put away that cannon." She smiled. "I assure you, I come in peace."

"That's good to know," Fargo replied. He walked over to the bed and placed the Colt under the pillow. He turned to look back at her, and she reached behind her and unbuttoned the back of her dress.

"I just thought I'd finish what I started this afternoon," she said, her lower lip full and moist, her eyes dusky with desire.

As her dress fell to the floor, Fargo saw that she

had made things easy for them both. She wore no corset or underclothes, not even a chemise. She stepped out of her slippers and strode boldly toward him. The dress had hid a lot—two saucy, upthrusting breasts with dark, nipples erect and ready, a waist so narrow he could span it with his hands, and a dark, gleaming pubic patch reaching between smooth white thighs.

He was naked himself by the time she reached him. He opened his arms to her. She walked boldly to him, pressing herself against his stiffness. He grabbed her buttocks and pulled her close. Like a key going into a lock, he entered her. His cock felt as if it were inside a furnace as she thrust her pelvis hungrily forward and flung her head back.

"Ever since this afternoon," she breathed, "I've been thinking of you. And all that . . . equipment."

"Is that why you left so quick?"

"What do *you* think?"

She ground her pubis into him, then leaned forward and pressed her breasts against his chest, letting her hair cascade down his back as she wrapped her arms about him.

"That's what I think," he said pulling them both up onto the bed. Rolling over onto her, he kept himself inside her, but held back from thrusting, savoring the feel of her hot muff tight around his erection and contenting himself for the moment by worrying her nipples with his tongue and teeth until they had grown so hard they were like hot nails.

Then he let his lips travel up to her neck and move behind her ears, nibbling for a while on each lobe. She was breathing heavily, frantically, as he closed his lips over hers and thrust his tongue deep into her mouth. Their tongues, hot and wanton, clashed feverishly.

She began to thrash and undulate wildly under him. But still he did not thrust as he kept her impaled beneath him, pinned to the bed, fighting her desperate desire to begin the thrusting. At last, she pulled her lips away from his.

"You bastard!" she cried fiercely.

Laughing, he pulled back. "What's the matter?"

"You know damn well!" She blew a wet lock of hair out of her eyes. "Get on with it! I can hardly move!"

He reached under her buttocks and lifted her off the bed, ramming her into him. Then he dropped her, allowing himself to slip out completely.

"No!" she groaned, gasping. "Stay in!"

"Make up your mind."

"Damn you!" she cried, arching up desperately to meet him.

By then he was no longer interested in prolonging things, either. He plunged down into her, this time hitting bottom as she grunted and drove back up against him like a coiled spring, meeting him thrust for thrust.

"Good!" she muttered. 'Yes, yes!"

Still thrusting, he reared upright, watching her fingers clutching at the blanket, her head turned to one side. He could see her mouth open and slack, her face pressing against the blanket with each heaving lunge, her eyes wide and staring.

He slowed then, teasing her again, moving back when she moved forward, denying her what she wanted.

"You bastard!" she snarled, looking back up at him.

Reaching up, she flung both arms around his neck, pulling him down onto her so she could claw at his back. He loved the feeling of her fingers on his back and resumed humping her with a happy, wild abandon.

"Keep going!" she whimpered. "Please. Don't stop."

This time he had no intention of stopping as he watched her breasts jiggling, her head straining back, her neck taut, her mouth open, and he felt his orgasm surging up relentlessly within him. At last he exploded inside her, pulsing wildly until, spent, he fell forward onto her breasts.

She shuddered and bucked like a bronc beneath him as she climaxed. When she finally went limp beneath him, he pulled her over onto her side and, with his big hands on her rear, pressed himself into her, ramming himself in deeply so as not to lose his erection.

Gasping, she flung her arms about him and squeezed him tightly. A moment later he could feel her trembling all over as she built to another climax . . . and another . . .

Sometime later, as their hard breathing began to slowly subside, they found themselves covered with a fine film of perspiration. The chill desert air was blowing in through the open window, so Fargo pulled a sheet over them both, then reached down for the bourbon.

"I could use some of that too," she said.

He pulled on the bottle a couple of times, then handed it to her. Wiping off the bottle's mouth with her palm, she took a healthy belt and handed it back to Fargo.

As he put it back down on the floor, she propped her head up on an elbow and peered at him, a gleam in her eyes. "I saw you out there tangling with Big John."

"That what they call Carswell?"

"Yep."

"Made a fool of myself."

"You tried to do the right thing. That took guts."

He looked at her. She dressed like a lady, fucked like a wildcat, and talked like a man. He shrugged. "That poor son of a bitch made it easy for everyone, I guess, when he broke away like that."

"You planning on staying in these parts, Fargo?"

"Nope."

"What brought you here in the first place?"

Fargo told her he was looking for a man called Silva, who he figured might have been mixed up in the attack on the mule team a couple of months ago in the Superstition Mountains.

"I remember Silva," she said. "He stayed at the hotel, but I didn't see much of him. He left with the mule team."

"The sheriff said he wasn't found with the others. Said he disappeared."

"He could have wandered off after the attack, wounded."

"Maybe."

"If he did, he wouldn't last long in that country."

"That ain't what I was thinkin'. Silva might've been in on that raise. And that could mean he's just the one I'm looking for."

"Why are you after him, Fargo? You're no lawman."

"Old business. There's four men I took after some time ago. Now there's just two left."

"And you're hopin' this is one of them."

Fargo nodded.

She looked at him for a long moment. "I see."

"You think I'm crazy?"

She shrugged. "You can spend your time playing pinochle with grizzly bears for all I care." She snuggled closer. "Say, where'd you get that funny half-moon scar on your arm?"

He grinned at her. "Playin' pinochle with grizzly bears."

"Be serious."

"I am. Almost. I got in a ruckus with a full-grown grizzly once. I was lucky I got away."

She shuddered and snuggled still closer. He held her close and asked how come she was the owner of a hotel out here in the middle of Apache country.

The hotel's original owner had given it to her father in payment for his silver mine, she told him. The silver petered out a few weeks after they signed the papers, making it the only good bargain she remembered her father ever having made. When he died a year later, he left the hotel in her name.

"So now you're stuck here?"

"You interested in buying?"

"Not on your life."

"Then you're right. I'm stuck here."

Fargo felt himself rising to the occasion once again. He must have been hornier than he realized. Too damn many days on the trail alone.

"Fargo?"

"What is it, Emma?"

"I don't think you should've got John Carswell all riled up like you did."

"Why not?"

"He might know something about Silva—or at least what happened to him."

"How so?"

"There's talk around that he had something to do with that lost silver shipment. One of his boys got drunk a few nights back and opened his mouth. His brother shut him up fast enough, but it's got some people in town talking. If Carswell *was* mixed up with that holdup, then maybe he would know what happened to Silva."

Fargo sat up and looked down at Emma Pool. "You might have something there. Carswell live in town?"

"No. He has a ranch under the Mogollon Rim, not far from the Superstition Mountains—and the Apaches."

"Ain't that a mite dangerous?"

"For the Apaches, maybe. There's talk in town that Carswell is in league with the Apaches. I wouldn't put it past him. That Carswell clan is wild; I wouldn't trust a single one of them. There's a passel of them, too—and they're as close as ticks on a hound dog."

"From what I know, the Mogollon Rim is near desert country."

"That's right, Skye."

"How can they make a living runnin' cattle on that kind of land?"

"That's what a lot of people wonder. Maybe they get a piece out of every mining camp or ranch the

Apaches loot. That's what the talk is, anyway. However they do it, they manage."

"And maybe hitting that pack train would be another way."

She nodded. "A lot of people are thinkin' that."

"Maybe I'll take a ride out to Clay Springs, Emma."

"When?"

"Soon."

"Well, not right now."

"No," he said, sinking down beside her. "Not right now."

She smiled and, reaching down into his crotch, closed her hand around his resurgent erection. Her eyes widened in pleased astonishment. "Now it's *my* turn to devil you," she told him, swinging one long limb over his waist.

"Go ahead. You've earned the right."

"You bet I have," she said, swinging the other leg over him.

Fargo said nothing as she rammed herself down as hard as she could onto his erection. He leaned back and prepared to enjoy himself. He had a long ride ahead of him the next day, but there was no way he would be able to leave first thing in the morning—not even if he wanted to. He was going to have too busy a night.

Not that he was complaining.

2

Fargo was in sight of the Mogollon Rim a little before noon the next day. Through the heat's shimmering curtain, the great, rugged escarpment loomed in the distance, appearing to Fargo like some massive wall flung up by ancient Titans. Beyond the rim, he knew, were the Apaches, and still farther beyond, the mysterious, craggy range known as the Superstition Mountains. But he wasn't worried about them now. The bright, baked land through which he was traveling on his way to Clay Springs was demanding all his attention.

The Ovaro shook his head unhappily and let it droop a few inches lower. Fargo didn't blame his mount. Hell's bells, he didn't feel so great himself as he rode on past these shimmering rock walls and baked, lifeless vegetation. His canteen was as dry as a pharaoh's tomb and neither he nor the pinto had seen fresh water since that morning.

Mopping his brow, he urged his pinto around a red,

towering rock, shaped by a million years of hot, sand-laden wind. Ahead, the shadowed mouth of a large canyon opened before him. He rode toward it gratefully.

Damn it! Who the hell is that?

Reining in, Fargo peered through the wavering heat. Far above him on the rim of the canyon a girl had appeared. Her hair was Indian black, her long green Spanish skirt and blouse so torn there was little left of either. She was waving frantically, desperately, to him. As he raised his arm to return her wave, a man came up behind her and dragged her struggling form from sight.

Yanking his pinto around toward a narrow game trail, Fargo urged it at a hard gallop up the steep slope toward the canyon rim.

Her name was Topaz. There was more Apache blood in her than Spanish, and it was the Spanish blood that gave her the blue eyes. All the rest of her—the long willowy figure, the sharp, uncomprising nose, and her capacity to fight—was Apache.

As Tom Carswell grabbed her by the hair and dragged her back down the trail after him, Topaz kicked out at him repeatedly, finally catching him with a nasty crack in the shins. When Tom bent with a cry to grab at his shin, Topaz reached up and raked his face, leaving a raw crescent of blood. Still clinging to her long hair, Tom brought up his six-gun and cracked her on the side of the head, sending her sprawling ahead of him down the rocky trail, all the way to the canyon floor.

She made no effort to get up, and Tom was certain

he had knocked her out. When he bent over her to sling her over his shoulder, she came alive instantly, striking him with the speed of a rattlesnake. Again she raked his face and her knee found his groin. He tried frantically to pull away, but she kept after him, her hard little fists punishing him about the face and head.

"Seth!" he called in weary resignation. "Seth! Get over here!"

Topaz kept after him, attempting to snatch the gun from his holster. He grabbed her hand to prevent this, and she sank her bright white teeth into the skin just above his knuckles. Howling, Seth stumbled back.

A shadow fell over Topaz. Before she could turn, Seth Carswell brought down the barrel of his six-gun onto her head.

The girl collapsed to the ground, unconscious.

Approaching her carefully, Tom studied her still figure, then stepped back and sent a vicious kick into her side.

Seth reached out to restrain him. "Pa wouldn't like that," he reminded Tom. "Don't forget, she's his woman now."

"She don't act like it."

"She will, when she gets used to it. It's just takin' a while to break her in, is all. Besides, Pa likes it when a girl shows grit. Makes it all the sweeter, he says."

Tom shook his head doubtfully. "I don't know. She sure is a hellcat. I don't trust her. She's mostly Apache. She'll kill us all in our sleep."

Seth shrugged. "She's what Pa wants, and that's that. He was sure as hell upset to find she'd got away. I'll get the horses."

Tom—his lean, freckled face burned raw from the sun—watched his brother move off down the canyon. Seth was a chunky fellow, little more than five feet five, as small and barrel-chested as Pa was tall and lanky. Yet he had all of Pa's instincts and was more than a match for either of his two brothers—at times, maybe even for Pa himself.

Tom looked over at the girl, still lying facedown in the full glare of the sun, her long black hair spilled over the ground about her head. As the sun made its trek across the cloudless sky, Tom walked over wearily to the girl. He made no attempt to carry her. Grabbing her by the hair, he dragged her across the canyon, looking for shade.

Once he found it, he dumped her unceremoniously onto the rocky ground. She rolled loosely and this time came to rest on her back, her legs spraddled, her face resting to one side. He gazed down at her, aware of the long scratches she had left on his face. He felt them gingerly, noting with alarm the faint, ridged scabs that were already forming.

Damn, fucking little hellcat he thought. Be a hell of a long time before them scars'd heal. Meanwhile, he'd be the laughingstock. Everyone in Tularo would be starin' at him, grinning too and askin' how he liked his pa's wildcat. And, goddammit, there was not a blamed thing he could do about it!

Topaz was his pa's latest attempt to find a woman to keep his house and warm his bed. The last one had lasted six years, the one before that ten. Sullen, foul-mouthed hags, both had been pussycats compared to this one. Pa had bought Topaz from an Apache who could no longer beat her into submission. And that wasn't hard for Tom to understand. On occasion, he had heard her blazing, withering oaths and knew she had a tongue that could lash a man clear to his soul, though for the most part she kept silent and let her blazing eyes speak for her.

She was pretty, though. Damn if she wasn't. He could understand his pa's hunger for her. Hell, at times he felt it himself. She pranced around without no corset and no underpants under her long skirt. And right now, her blouse was so torn he could see most all of one breast, nipple and all. It was spilled out so beautiful white, it made him sweat to gaze on it.

He blinked and looked suddenly around. What he was thinking was not something he wanted his pa to find out about. But hell, who was gonna tell? She was unconscious. She wouldn't know a thing about it! He stepped out of the shade and looked down the canyon. Seth was nowhere in sight. Hell, he'd be a while yet, especially in this blasted heat. They'd left their horses at least half a mile farther down the canyon.

Tom looked back down at Topaz, licked his suddenly dry lips, and slipped his wide yellow suspenders off his shoulders . . .

Fargo reached the rim of the canyon. It was going to be difficult to pinpoint where the girl and the man who had grabbed her had been standing, he realized. Every landmark that had stood out so clearly from the trail below now assumed a totally different aspect once he pulled to a halt atop the canyon's rim.

To the right of his pinto, a steep-sided canyon wall dropped away. Though he was not yet in the Superstition Mountains, he figured this patch of hell was a good hint of what lay within that forbidding range. On all sides of him extended a wilderness of vaulting, striated towers of rock and intimidating brows of overhanging ledges and boulders, some reddish in tint, others gleaming blades of basalt as smooth as glass, while over it all hung the numbing, shriveling heat of midday.

He glanced down at the canyon floor, urged his pinto toward a game trail, and soon found signs of a struggle that had taken place there. Following footprints and the wobbly tracks left by a pair of bootheels being dragged along, he nudged his pinto carefully down the steep, talus-littered trail.

When he gained the canyon floor, he dismounted. Hunkering down, he studied the signs carefully, clearly reading the struggle. He straightened and, leading his pinto, followed the tracks of a man moving off down the canyon. He was dragging someone—the girl he had glimpsed from the trail probably—across the canyon. Fargo followed the tracks through the blazing sunlight to the far side of the canyon. Cutting around a shoulder of rock, he pulled up, amazed at the scene before him.

The girl Fargo had glimpsed earlier was sprawled on the ground, unconscious. A filthy, gangling youth of twenty or so was crouched over her, his britches on the ground behind him. What fascinated Fargo was the man's long, thin erection, slightly bent at the tip. It looked ludicrous, and if the girl were not unconscious, Fargo was sure she would have been heaping scorn on his ridiculous equipment.

Fargo dropped the reins of his pinto and unlimbered his six-gun, cocking it as he did so. The sound was sharp enough to cause the young man to fling himself around. When he saw Fargo, he gasped and backed up hastily.

Looking at him face on, Fargo noted at once the resemblance to Big John Carswell. So this was one of his boys—one of his bad boys. Fargo stepped closer. "I ought to blow off that pencil you call a dick, mister."

"No! Please!"

"Give me one good reason."

"Look, there's no need for that. We can share her."

"*Share* her?"

"Sure!"

"She's unconscious. What's the matter with you? You like layin' corpses?"

The fellow's face went pale and took another step back. "No need to get all riled. This here's Topaz. She ain't nothin' but a half-breed."

"You mean she's part Indian."

He nodded quickly. "Apache and Mex. That's all she is."

"You white all the way?"

"Sure," he replied, sniffing with sudden pride. "I sure as hell ain't no mixbreed."

Fargo smiled, his brilliant white teeth in sharp contrast to his tanned, eaglelike face. "I'm part Indian, mister. Can't you tell lookin' at me?" As he spoke, Fargo took off his hat. "Take a look."

When the fellow saw Fargo's thick shock of ink-black hair, Fargo thought he was going to shit. Beads of sweat stood out on his forehead and he took another step backward. "Jesus Christ, feller, I didn't mean nothin' by that."

"No. 'Course you didn't.'"

But Fargo's anger was fading fast, giving way to disgust. The scrawny fellow's erection had shrunk into a sad little finger, barely visible in his filthy crotch. Holstering his gun, Fargo told him to get dressed.

As Fargo turned to go back for his pinto, he found himself looking into the muzzle of a Colt, held in the right hand of a broad-shouldered, tough-looking hombre. The resemblance to the lanky one was undeniable, however, and Fargo realized this was another of Carswell's sons.

"Good thing you put away that iron, mister," the newcomer said.

Fargo did not reply.

The smaller man looked past Fargo at his brother. His face was grim. "I'd a shot you, Tom—soon's I got this one—if I'd seen you humpin' Topaz. Go on now and do like the man said. Put your britches back on. You're embarrassing the shit out of me."

"Dammit, Seth! That little spitfire came at me somethin' awful back there," Tom protested, stepping hastily into his pants. "I just wanted to give her something she'd remember me by."

"You ain't got nothin' to give that one, boy—and besides, she's Pa's woman. You're lucky this here man stopped you or Pa would've had your hide."

"Topaz wouldn't have knowed a thing, Seth!"

"Jesus!" Seth said, looking in weary exasperation away from his brother. "Sure, he's my kin," he admitted, glancing at Fargo. "But don't blame me for that."

"I won't."

"Seth Carswell's the name. My fool brother there is Tom," the man said.

"Fargo. Sky Fargo," the Trailsman replied.

"You'll be comin' with us. Pa'll stand you to a bed and good grub."

"You sure of that?"

"Why wouldn't he?"

Fargo smiled. John Carswell would do nothing of the sort. But Seth had no way of knowing that.

"All right, Seth. Thanks for the invite."

They made their way through the blistering afternoon heat. The girl had regained consciousness before they started out and done a pretty good job of rearranging her torn skirt and blouse to cover most of her charms—though sure as hell not all of them. A horse had been brought for her and she rode alongside Fargo, a sullen, glowering woman who rode her mount better than either of the two brothers trailing them. She and Fargo were able to communicate only through occasional glances, but Fargo had no difficulty making it clear to her that he was on her side. And she must have remembered waving frantically down at him for that brief instant.

At last the badlands dropped away behind them, and Fargo felt the land lifting under him. After a while, they reached the cooler, timber-clad flanks of the foothills closing about them. It was close to dusk when the Carswell ranch came in sight—a sprawling outfit spread among some cottonwood and pine. The main building looked like one long room built of logs, with an adobe wing built on the south end serving as the bunkhouse. A cluster of sheds and corrals lay off to the north at the edge of the sprawling compound.

They were well up in the tableland now. The tall timber at the rear of the ranchhouse had been cut down, but higher on the slopes shouldering steeply away from the ranch, ponderosa pine were mixed in with the heavy timber. The faint, but cooler breeze at this elevation brought with it the tang of pine needles.

As soon as they were clearly in sight of the ranch buildings, Fargo heard a cry and a moment later saw John Carswell emerge from the main house, a rifle in his hand. He strode off the porch and hurried across the compound toward them, issuing sharp orders to his hands. At once they appeared from the surrounding barns and sheds, as another of Carswell's sons hurried out of the ranchhouse, a rifle in his hand also.

When Carswell was close enough to recognize Fargo, his lean blade of a face cracked into a wolfish grin. "We meet again, Mr. Fargo."

"Just Fargo will be fine, Carswell."

"Will it, now?"

Carswell glanced at Seth. "Where'd you find Mr. Fargo here?"

"He was with Tom and Topaz at Red Canyon. He was keepin' Tom honest, Pa."

"That so?" Carswell glanced coldly at Tom, then came to a halt beside Fargo's pinto, the muzzle of his rifle yawning up at Fargo. "What're you after, Mr. Fargo?"

"I've come this far from Tularo just to see you, Carswell."

"Well, now, ain't that somethin'! Welcome to the Lazy C. There ain't no one has ever questioned Carswell hospitality." He stepped back and lowered his rifle. "Light and set a spell. I just got back myself not too long ago."

As Fargo dismounted, Carswell turned his attention to the girl. "When you goin' to learn, Topaz?" he demanded of her. "You can't get away from here. Not on foot, anyway. This here country's too tough, even for you."

She glared down at him for a long moment without saying a thing, then looked away, her gaze straight ahead—at the Mogollon Rim, possibly thinking of what lay beyond.

"I ain't goin' to beat on you, not this time," Carswell assured her. "But you better mind from here on in. I paid a good price for you, gave your man plenty of goods."

Topaz glanced quickly down at Carswell, her eyes blazing. For a moment Fargo thought she was going to spit in Carswell's face. But she held her rage in check and looked away from him, her fierce eyes glowing.

Carswell reached up to take her hand. Topaz pulled it away defiantly, then slipped from the saddle as easily as any Indian and brushed past him, heading for the ranchhouse. A squat, round Indian housekeeper, easily twice her age, hurried anxiously out to intercept her. But when she grabbed Topaz's arm, Topaz pulled free and swept on past her into the house.

With a conscious effort to hold in his chagrin at Topaz's behavior, Carswell turned to Fargo and managed a cold smile.

"We'll be settin' down to supper soon, Mr. Fargo. I'll let you take care of that pretty Ovaro of yours. You're welcome to the pump out back. Seth here'll be glad to show you around the place." He turned to Seth and winked. "Won't you, son?"

"I sure will, Pa," said Seth, grinning openly.

Carswell was as good as his word. The meal placed down before Fargo was a good one. As Fargo leaned back in his chair to light the cheroot Carswell handed him and allow the two women to clear off the table, he looked calmly about him at his hosts.

There had been little conversation during the meal, as was usual on a working ranch. But all through the meal, Carswell's three sons were watching like wolf cubs, waiting for their pa to make the first killing swipe. The youngest of Carswell's sons was called Billy Joe. He was the unhealthiest-looking of the three, with hair that resembled rotting hay and a vacant, idiot gleam in his green eyes that chilled Fargo.

"That was a fine meal, Carswell," Fargo said, puffing contentedly on his cigar. "My compliments to the cooks."

"That'd be Moon Face," Carswell drawled. "I don't let Topaz near the food . . . yet."

"A wise precaution," Fargo commented.

"You said you came out here to see me. What for?"

"I want to know more about Federico Silva—and the heist of that silver shipment."

"What makes you think I'd know more than anyone else?"

Fargo shrugged. "There's been some talk in Tularo. And just a feeling I have about you and your boys."

"You want to explain that?"

"You live well, damn well, for a rancher, but I didn't see any beef cattle on my way here."

"That so?" Carswell glanced quickly around at his

three sons, one eyebrow canting demoniacally. "Well, don't let it worry you none. I shipped most of my cattle to market this spring before the grass all dried up. Sold 'em to the army for a good price. Maybe you ain't heard. They got a war goin' on back East."

"I heard."

"I ain't goin' to deny I knowed Silva, though. He stopped by here on his way through to the Superstitions. Never saw him again, though. I figure the Apaches of the sun got him. It don't matter which. You sure he's the one you're after."

Fargo described the man he had been searching for these many years. Carswell agreed it fit Silva's description. Then he leaned back in his chair and eyed Fargo coldly for a moment. "You a lawman?" he asked finally.

Fargo shook his head. But he could see that Carswell didn't believe him.

"Then, what's your interest in that shipment?"

"It's Silva I'm after. Not the shipment. Nothing for you to worry about, if you had nothing to do with the heist. Or Silva's disappearance."

"I didn't," drawled Carswell, "and neither did any of these three cottonheads sitting beside me."

"Then maybe you could tell me how to reach the spot where the shipment was stopped. If Silva's still alive, I might pick up his trail from there."

"You sure want that bastard bad, don't you?" said Billy Joe, leaning forward eagerly, his eyes glittering. "What'd he do, murder someone?"

"Shut up, Billy Joe," Carswell said.

"Where was the mule team attacked?" Fargo asked.

"Chimney Rock," blurted Tom. "Them Apaches came down on them wagons at Chimney Rock."

"Shut up, Tom," snapped John Carswell. "We don't know that for certain."

"Why, sure, Pa. Don't you remember—"

"I said, shut up." Carswell reached over and snatched him by the wrist.

Tom winced in sudden pain and pulled away. "Oh, sure, Pa! I forgot."

Carswell smiled at Fargo. "Just can't keep a fool young'un from speakin' out a turn, seems like. Sorry, Mr. Fargo. All we know for sure is that mule team was attacked deep in the mountains."

"Yeah," said Seth, grinning slyly, "deep in the Superstitions."

Fargo stood up. "Well, Carswell, I thank you for the supper—and now, if you'll excuse me, I think I'll get me some shut-eye."

"There's a room in the barn," said Carswell. "You can sleep in there. Seth will show you the way. Plenty of straw for a bed in there and the privy's real close."

"Much obliged," Fargo said, lifting his hat off the hook by the door.

He paused for a moment to glance over at Topaz. She was dipping a dish into a wooden bucket. As soon as she caught his glance, he touched his hat brim to her, then stepped out into the already chilly night, Seth Carswell right behind him.

The horses in their stalls on the other side of the partition were stamping restlessly. But they had not awakened Fargo. Instead, it was the creak of the door behind him leading to the outside. Slowly, carefully, he removed his Colt from under his pillow and braced himself as light footfalls moved steathily closer across the board floor.

He was about to whip around with his gun cocked when a deft hand lifted his blanket and a warm, lithe body slipped in behind him, snuggling quickly up against his long frame. Turning his head, he saw himself looking into Topaz's light-blue eyes. She smiled, her bright white teeth gleaming in the darkness. Her fingers played lightly over his face and came to rest on his mouth, pressing the lips together gently.

"Shh," she said. "We be quiet. Or the old one will be in here with a shotgun, you bet."

Her appraisal of his predicament was right on target. But he did not hesitate as he made room on the straw for her. She stayed with him, flattening her warm body against his, her hot hand reaching over and down to close about his sudden erection. With a soft, eager grunt, she snuggled still closer. He gave up and turned around to face her, and she rammed her warm muff against his erection, lifting one leg just enough to let him enter.

Shoving his Colt back under the pillow, he grabbed her buttocks and rammed into her as far as he could.

"Ah, this is good," she murmured. "I wait long time for real man! Too long!"

"Shut up," Fargo told her. "You got what you came in here for, so quiet down and take it—all of it!"

She grunted in savage agreement, grabbed his shoulders, and pulled him over onto her, thrusting eagerly up at him as she did so. Fargo considered a bit more foreplay, but Topaz appeared to be in a real hurry. Besides, there was really no need for him to heat up the oven. Topaz was already well-lubricated, and before long was writhing under him like a wildcat, her fingers raking down his back, opening up the scratches Emma Poole had left and creating fresh ones.

If this sort of punishment kept up much longer, Fargo figured, he'd be out of skin before long.

He was humping happily and had almost reached his orgasm when she began exploding beneath him, laughing softly up at him with each violent spasm. She sure as hell had a short fuse.

But he sure as hell was not finished yet.

At once she realized his dilemma.

"Now I ride you!" she hissed.

She pushed him back and forked a thigh over him, then plunged recklessly down upon him, riding him with a furious, ecstatic abandon. Fargo tightened his buttocks and drove up to meet each wild, furious thrust. She began twisting her head from side to side, her long black hair exploding out behind her, her teeth clenched, a kind of mewing groan coming from deep within her. Running both hands over her breasts, he felt the lovely softness of her silken skin.

Soon, however, there was no more deliberation. He had bought himself a ticket, found a seat, and now the train was rushing down the track—a greased track to perdition or heaven, it didn't matter which. He was only dimly aware of her pleased chuckle as he bucked high in his first orgasm, carrying both of them over the top, the delicious release washing him clean as it swept her along with him.

At last, sweat oozing from each pore, he sank back on the straw, spent. Laughing softly, Topaz flung her arms about him and collapsed forward onto his chest, resting her cheek on his thick mat of coiled hair. As he regained his breath, he stroked her long hair. Lifting her head after a while, she looked into his eyes, then began kissing his lips with a violent, sweaty, passionate intensity. He was still erect and had kept himself inside her. Suddenly he could feel her pulsing repeatedly as she continued to experience a rapid series of quiet, seemingly involuntary orgasms.

"Ummm," she murmured at last as she quieted with a sigh. Spreading her legs slightly, she pulled back and released him. "I could not stop. You make me alive again."

He chuckled softly, kissed her fluttering eyelids, and brushed back her gleaming mantle of black hair, aware of the fine beads of perspiration covering her features.

She buried her face in the hollow of his neck. "I know you be this nice," she murmured. "I see it in your eyes when first you look on me."

"Come here," he said softly, rolling over and pulling her closer, aware that he was still very much alive.

But she pushed him gently back. "No. Is enough for now. I come to warn you!"

"Warn me?"

"Yes."

"About what?"

"Carswell send his sons here to kill you before morning. Then he go after the silver shipment you and him talk about."

"Hold on a minute. You're going too fast for me."

"After you leave, I hear them talk. The old man not believe you. He say must be lawman. So he wait no longer. He say Billy Joe and Seth must kill you this night. Then they decide who get your pretty horse and go after the silver."

"You mean Carswell knows where it is?"

She nodded. "That one you seek. Carswell think maybe *he* has it."

"Federico Silva?"

"Yes. Federico, he supposed to hide it, then come back to tell old man where. But Silva, he not come back. Maybe Apache kill him, maybe not. But Carswell say he will find him. He say Silva is the son of a female dog and he will wait for him no more."

Fargo sat up. His erection had vanished completely. "Dammit, Topaz! You should have told me this sooner."

She smiled, her teeth flashing in the darkness. "I want you first. I am hungry for a man—a big man. I dream of such a man as you. For too long, I not feel such a big man inside me. My need is like a fire that burns."

"I sure as hell hope I've quenched it."

"Yes, you have," she admitted, "for now."

"I'm lighting out, Topaz, and leaving you here."

She sat up, her eyes fixing him sternly. "No. You must take me with you. They will kill me when they find I warn you."

"I'll come back for you."

"I tell you no. Already I have saddle your horse, the beautiful Ovaro. And my paint. We go now—and we go together."

"I travel alone, Topaz."

She shook her head emphatically. "This time you go with me, or you not go. I not tell you where I hide your horse. And I will stand in the darkness and watch them kill you."

He looked into her eyes and saw neither anger nor compassion, only the look of a very healthy female animal ready to spring in whichever direction her survival dictated.

"All right," he told her. "But we leave now." He lit the small lamp hanging on a nail over his cot.

She stood up. "Dress. I will take you to the horses."

She stepped into a long Spanish skirt, this one black, and a fresh white blouse. Fargo dressed as quickly and was reaching for the door when it was flung open. Seth and Billy Joe stood hesitantly at the doorway, startled at finding Fargo upright and dressed.

That pause was fatal.

Topaz lunged past Fargo. He saw something flash in her hand—a long blade—and heard Billy Joe squeal out in sudden pain. Lowering his shoulder, Fargo bowled both men back into the night. As Billy Joe sprawled to the ground, Fargo stepped over him and brought his gunbarrel around hard, catching Seth against the side of the head. He went flying backward, slammed into the ground, and lay still.

Topaz paused only long enough to kick the moaning Billy Joe into silence, then darted swiftly up the slope. Fargo followed after her and in a few minutes reached the waiting horses. Topaz was astride her paint in one swift leap, pulling up the slope ahead of him before he had stepped into his saddle. He spurred after her through the darkness, listening for any sign of pursuit.

But he heard nothing. He glanced up at the night sky. It was a moonless night. They were in luck.

3

They rode the rest of that night and all through the next day, camping at last under a red cliff beside a water hole filled by a steady trickle oozing through a crack in the rock. Topaz had led him unerringly to the water, telling him an hour or so after they would reach it at sundown.

And they had.

They were well into the Superstition Mountains by this time and Fargo was impressed by the stark, somber sprawl of rock and brush, the twisting canyons and arroyos, the utter desolation. Not long after he entered the mountains, he became aware that without Topaz's assistance, he would never be able to make it back the way he had come. If Carswell and his sons had been on their trail at the beginning of this day, they were sure as hell on it no longer. No one could have followed the tortuous route Topaz had taken, a route it was obvious she had taken before. And she was doing more than helping Fargo to escape Carswell.

She had something else in mind, and Fargo sensed it had little to do with him or Carswell.

Having drunk his fill and seen to his pinto, Fargo was sitting in the fading light, his back against the base of the cliff, watching Topaz. Their last meal of the day was finished and had consisted of meager portions of hardtack and jerky he had stored in his saddlebag. After the supper tins had been washed and put away, Topaz had taken off her clothes and bathed in the water hole. Now, fully clothed once more, she was combing out her long black hair.

"Where're we going, Topaz?"

Without stopping the smooth stroking of her hair, she turned to look at him. "What do you mean? I take you from Carswell."

"You know what I mean. You're heading somewhere special. And it looks like I'm just along for the ride."

She shrugged and continued to comb out her hair. "I know a man like me. He is half-breed too. He is good rancher. He will protect me from the old man, Carswell."

"He got a name?"

"Ken Santana. Now I am no more slave of Carswell, I think maybe I will be Santana's woman."

He looked at her for a long moment. She was very beautiful. All of a sudden Fargo almost found himself envying this rancher, Santana. "How far is his ranch from here?"

"Another day's ride. South of these mountains."

"Topaz, Tom mentioned Chimney Rock. He said that was where the mule train was attacked. You think maybe you could show me where that is."

"I show you. After I see Ken Santana."

Fargo nodded wearily. "Then we'd better get some sleep."

He got to his feet to fetch his sleeping bag. As he moved past her, she looked up at him.

"Tonight I will visit you. If you want."

"Save yourself," he told her, "for that feller Santana."

"He not save himself for me, but if you are too weary . . ." She shrugged.

Fargo hated to admit it, but she was right. Only he wasn't just weary. He was blown out, as empty as a corn husk tumbling in the wind. He couldn't believe Topaz's stamina. Or her capacity. Made a man humble, it sure did.

Without replying, he continued on past her to where he had stashed his bedroll.

They left the Superstitions about midday and just before sundown reached Ken Santana's small one-man ranch high in the forested foothills. As they rode in through the pole gate, a man Fargo assumed to be Santana stepped out of his log ranch building and stood for a moment on the low porch, shading his eyes. When he saw who it was riding alongside Fargo, he left the porch and hurried across the yard to greet him.

Before he reached them, Topaz slipped off her horse and flung herself into his arms. "I have come back," she told him. "Now I stay here with you."

"But I thought Teenaro sold you to Big John!"

She stepped back and tossed her head haughtily. "You think I let that old man touch me?" She turned then to present Fargo. "This man Fargo help me escape, so I am Carswell's no longer. Now I stay with you." She smiled provocatively at him. "You want?"

For answer he stepped closer and drew her hungrily to him. His kiss was long and hard, and Topaz responded. Fargo guessed that settled it. It was obvious Ken Santana was more than pleased at Topaz's sudden arrival.

Santana released Topaz, his face darkening self-consciously as he looked up at Fargo. "Light and rest, Mr. Fargo," he said. "And thanks for bringing Topaz back."

Fargo dismounted and shook Santana's hand. "It was more like Topaz bringing me. She saved me considerable trouble. Carswell had some ugly plans for me."

"Sounds like Carswell. Come inside out of this sun," Santana said, turning and leading them back to his ranchhouse.

Watching the man precede him across the yard, Fargo judged him to be taller and certainly leaner than any Apache, but his dark complexion and the set of his eyes, along with the inky blackness of his hair, left no doubt that—like Fargo—Indian blood flowed in his veins.

The interior of his small ranchhouse was tidy enough, and the moment Fargo saw the armchair with the buffalo robe thrown over it, he headed for it and slumped wearily down. He was saddle-sore and famished, and he could smell the pot of tea Santana had boiling on the wood stove in the corner. The tea's aroma compensated for the heat the stove generated—that and the way the big armchair closed gently about his big sore frame.

Santana poured tea into a large tin mug, mixed in a large dollop of honey, and handed it to Fargo. Sipping the hot tea, Fargo found it sweet, but bracing. He leaned luxuriously back in the armchair as Santana and Topaz made themselves comfortable on the couch across from him. They sat very close and Fargo could tell they were damn near close to igniting.

"How come you found yourself in Carswell's clutches?" Ken Santana asked, smiling encouragingly. "Topaz had no choice. Teenaro sold her to that old bastard. Who sold you?"

Fargo laughed, then told him of his search for Federico Silva and his curiosity concerning the missing silver shipment that had led him to search out Carswell. Then Topaz related how she had waved in desperation to Fargo when Tom Carswell was overtaking her. She finished up with her helping Fargo to escape, leaving out a few, somewhat intimate details in the process.

"Chimney Rock, you say?" Ken Santana mused, addressing Fargo. "I know where that is, and I've heard about that holdup, too."

"I take Fargo to Chimney Rock," Topaz said.

Fargo smiled at her. "I'd sure appreciate it, Topaz."

"But for now," said Santana, "you are my guest."

"Of course." Fargo sipped the tea. "By the way, you wouldn't happen to have something to go with this tea, would you?"

Santana grinned. "I have just the thing," he said, striding over to a wall cabinet.

When he returned with a bottle of Kentucky bourbon, Fargo knew he was going to enjoy this visit with Ken Santana, even if he could no longer enjoy his woman.

* * *

"There," Topaz said, pointing. "Follow that canyon for one day and you will come to river. Follow river upstream another day. There you will see Chimney Rock."

It was three days later, and Topaz had ridden out with him quite early in the morning so as to escape the heat of the day. Now they were astride their mounts on a ridge overlooking the Superstition Mountains. Fargo saw the canyon Topaz had just indicated and her directions seemed simple enough.

He glanced at Topaz. "Maybe I should ride back a ways with you."

"You not need to, Skye," she replied, smiling. "I will not get lost."

"No, I don't think you could, at that. But I keep thinking about Carswell. He's not the kind to sit still for what we did."

She smiled. "Ken and Topaz, we part Apache, don't forget. We know how to fight as good as any white-eyes."

Fargo grinned back at her. "And you can do something else as good or better than any white woman."

Topaz laughed, and standing up in her saddle, she leaned over and wrapped one arm around Fargo's neck, kissing him on the lips, stirring the embers to life within him. Smiling and obviously aware of what she had just done to him, she sat back down on her paint, wheeled the animal, and started back.

She did not get far before she held up and called out sharply to Fargo, pointing at the horizon.

When he rode back and pulled up alongside her, he saw the dim smudge against the southern horizon. The smoke was not shifting or moving along, as it would have if it were a grass or a forest fire. It was staying put, pumping a steady dark plume into the hot sky.

What was burning was a dwelling of some sort—or a barn.

Topaz gasped. "The ranch!" she cried.

At once the two spurred back the way they had come.

Santana's ranchhouse and his barn were only smoking embers by the time they reached it. Even the corral fences had been pulled down. The prints of unshod Indian ponies were everywhere.

They found Ken Santana in the brush in back of a burnt-out shed. His rifle had brought down two Apaches, and his skinning knife had disemboweled still another. The black shafts of two Apache arrows protruded from his ribs. But he was still alive. Barely.

With a terrible cry, Topaz flung herself beside him.

Feebly, Santana stroked Topaz's head. Looking past her at Fargo, he whispered, "Teenaro . . . he asked where Topaz was. I wouldn't tell him."

"Was Carswell with him?"

He shook his head slightly. "No. But Carswell sent him," he managed.

Ken Santana began to cough then, his long frame twitching painfully. Each paroxysm caused his face to twist in agony, and when at last the coughing faded, so did the light in his eyes. His head fell back loosely. Sobbing terribly, Topaz still clung to him, her cheek held against his.

Abruptly she pulled away, looked down at his slack, lifeless face, and with a terrible, keening cry, began ripping at her dress and pulling out handfuls of her hair. Fargo wrapped his arms around her, pinning her arms to restrain her. Then, lifting her bodily, he carried her back toward their horses. She fought him bitterly all the way and he had all he could do to hold on to her. But at last she regained some control and he released her. Sobbing weakly, she dropped to the ground.

"I will kill Teenaro," she said finally, her voice low, sounding almost as if it belonged to someone else. "With my own hands I will kill him. Then I will kill Carswell for sending Teenaro."

Listening to her, Fargo had no doubt that if Topaz ever got the opportunity, she would make good her vow.

The next morning Fargo found himself looking up at a bright morning sky. He and Topaz had buried Santana the night before, the memory of Topaz's terrible grief still burned into his consciousness.

Something was wrong. Flinging aside his blanket, he sat up and looked over to where Topaz had curled up the night before. She was gone. Jumping to his feet, he pulled on his boots and began packing his bedroll. A moment later he was mounted up, following Topaz's tracks north.

She was pushing the paint, and Fargo was unable to overtake her in the hammering heat. By midafternoon, he knew he was deep in Apache country, and when he topped a rise a little before sundown, he saw Topaz ahead of him about a mile, heading down a long draw. And that was not all he saw. Four Apaches were riding down the draw toward her.

Dismounting, Fargo pulled his pinto back off the

ridge, then crouched behind a clump of bushes to watch.

Topaz did not slow her paint. Holding up her hand in greeting, she rode directly toward the approaching Apaches. The Apaches pulled up and waited for her. When she reached them, they surrounded her. Offering no resistance, she continued on down the draw, escorted by the Apaches. Dimly visible on the horizon beyond the draw, Fargo saw the smoke of an Apache encampment.

Fargo waited until it was dark before following.

When he came to within a few hundred yards of the Apache village, he tethered his pinto in a draw and approached stealthily through the night until he was less than fifty yards from the village. The moonless night was alive with fires and the steady beat of drums. Occasional shouts rent the night. A celebration was in progress.

Like a large snake, Fargo eased himself through the brush, his bowie knife in his teeth. Reaching finally the outermost ring of shabby wickiups, he peered beyond them at the frenzied activity inside the encampment. The first thing he noticed was the appalling smell, then the sad squalor of the place. Instead of hides, filthy, torn army blankets were used to cover most of the wickiups.

And everywhere Fargo looked he saw the flat, impassive faces of the People, with their wide cheekbones, square jaws, their black, sullen eyes peering out from under cruel brows. Because of their wide shoulders and deep chests, the men, wearing breechclouts and their traditional, high-topped moccasins, seemed shorter than they actually were. For the most part the braves were sinewy and powerful, their long black hair falling to their shoulders, a simple headband holding it in place.

Naked children ranged freely, slashing at hoops with sticks, their excited shouts blending in with the steady chanting and drumbeating that came from the center of the camp, where a great bonfire blazed.

Fargo spotted Topaz. Still wearing her black skirt and white blouse, she was pushing her way through a small crowd, an Apache warrior close on her heels. Her face was grimly triumphant.

Fargo guessed the warrior behind her was Teenaro, the husband who had sold her to Carswell. He had the look of a savage who has just won a great prize or taught someone a lesson they deserved. As he and Topaz passed through the crowd of Indians, the watching Apaches dug one another with their elbows and cried out to them, lifting their earthen mugs of mescal in salute.

To everyone in the camp—including Teenaro, her ex-husband—Topaz had returned to her lord and master and made her peace with him.

Fargo watched the two disappear into the night, heading for a wickiup apart from the others on the far side of the village. Fargo ducked back into the night and, keeping low, circled the encampment. He reached the wickiup just in time to see Topaz and Teenaro disappear inside.

Fargo crept stealthily toward the wickiup and with his bowie silently sliced a slit through the blanket and the thin layer of brush that covered it, and watched.

Topaz had moved well back into the wickiup, past the small fire still glowing in the hearth until she was squatting beside Teenaro's low cot. Then she peeled off her blouse and reached down to unbutton the side of her skirt. Fargo saw Teenaro watching her closely as she undressed, his face gleaming with triumph. He had his woman back, and Fargo knew he would show her who was master.

Flinging off his breechclout, Teenaro rushed upon her like a rutting buck. Topaz barely had time to fling aside her skirt. Taking her by the shoulders, Teenaro threw her onto his cot, then flung himself atop her naked body, roughly wedging his knee between her thighs, spreading her for his entry.

Topaz closed her eyes and submitted. Grunting like a pig, Teenaro began his thrusting. Topaz was doing her best to simulate passion, waiting for the right moment to seek her revenge, Fargo figured.

Teenaro's rutting grew even more frantic. He pounded at her with a savage, headlong beat, lost completely in his effort to bring himself to come. As he neared his climax, he flung his head back, shaking loose his tangled, greasy hair. At last he came, crying out in savage exultation.

The frenzy of his coming turned him savage. He reached down and grabbed Topaz's hair and began slamming her head down again and again, all the while continuing to pump into her in a frenzied, futile attempt to retain his erection.

Fargo began to slice through the wickiup. Topaz's plan had gone far enough, he figured. He'd take care of the greasy Indian himself.

By now, Topaz had reached up and pulled Teenaro's hands from her hair as she rolled out from under him, his soft erection slipping out easily as she did so.

Teenaro was enraged. Furious, he snatched up his knife, which was lying on the floor of the wickiup, and lunged at her. The blade caught Topaz under her right breast and slashed her all the way to her right side, opening up a neat flap of skin that immediately began oozing blood.

His slicing complete, Fargo plunged through the wickiup, and vaulted in, leaping at the startled Teenaro. The Apache ducked and Fargo went sprawling. When he turned in the narrow place and tried to get up, Teenaro dropped upon his chest, his knees pinning Fargo to the ground. With a triumphant cry, Teenaro raised his knife over his head.

Topaz flung himself at Teenaro and caught his wrist with both hands, slowing Teenaro's downward stroke. The knife missed Fargo's head and sank into the ground beside him. Before the Apache could withdraw his knife, Fargo slashed upward with his bowie.

Teenaro gasped, then looked down in wide-eyed wonder at the hilt of Fargo's knife protruding from his bowels. Already, a black trickle of blood was oozing out around the blade. He looked over at Topaz, then back to Fargo, and in that instant he knew he had been betrayed. Pitching forward onto the dirt floor, he twitched once, twice, then settled onto his side, breathing his last.

Pushing him over, Fargo retrieved his knife and wiped it clean on the Apache's thigh, then turned his attention to Topaz.

She did not look good. The shock of what she had experienced was beginning to show in the sudden pallor of her face and the thin sheen of perspiration covering it. By this time her wound was bleeding profusely, covering her entire right side with a dark, gleaming wash of fresh blood. Swiftly, Fargo snatched down a buckskin dress hanging from an antler and ripped it into strips, then bound her about the waist, managing to staunch the flow.

"We can't stay here," he told her.

"I can," she said. "But you must go."

"I'm not leaving without you."

"No. I am wounded. I will only slow you down. Besides, you have done for me what I came to do." She smiled wanly. "I am content that Teenaro is dead. Go now."

"Hell, Topaz, how'm I going to find Chimney Rock? I need you to come with me."

"But I will need a horse."

"We'll use mine. Ride double. Come on. We don't have time to argue."

Without further protest, Topaz stood up and struggled into her skirt and blouse, then pushed out ahead of him through the hole in the wickiup's side, but not before delivering one final, slashing kick to the dead Apache's head.

The mescal-fueled celebration was in full swing, the steady drumming filling the night with an ominous beat, as Fargo hoisted the wounded Topaz up onto the saddle in front of him and turned the pinto toward the Superstition Mountains.

At daybreak, many miles into the mountains, he stopped by a water hole to examine Topaz's wound. He did not like what he saw. Along its entire length the flesh on both sides looked raw and inflamed and was extremely sensitive to the touch. The wound itself was festering, and though Fargo did his best to clean it out with fresh water, he knew his efforts were inadequate. What he needed was some whiskey to flush it out thoroughly. He had never believed what doctors said, that there was such a thing as laudable pus; any time he had seen pus in a wound, it presaged terrible suffering and many times death—and already there was too much of it in Topaz's wound.

Without uttering a sound of complaint, Topaz endured his primitive attempt to clean out her wound. When he had done all he could, they set out again through the twisting canyons and arroyos, heading toward Chimney Rock. Topaz had insisted that she show it to him, and Fargo had decided it would do no harm to humor her.

Two days later, by nightfall, it was clear she could go on no farther.

Fargo made camp by a stream, their backs to a rock wall. He built a fire, but in the chill desert air, Topaz began to shake all over. He wrapped her burning body in blankets and his bedroll to keep out the chill, but her teeth continued to chatter uncontrollably, and when he tried to examine her wound, she would not let him.

"It hurt too much," she told him.

"But I've got to clean it out."

"Please . . . it does not matter."

"But you'll die."

She smiled wanly. "I am already dead."

He tried to think of a rejoinder, but nothing occurred to him. She had accepted her fate and was now looking death in the eye without blinking or flinching away. He had to respect that kind of courage, so he busied himself piling clothing and blankets onto her, more to keep himself busy than for any hope he had that it would do her any good.

At last he contented himself with holding her close in his arms, hoping that the added heat of his body might at least banish some of the terrible chill that racked her. But she continued to shiver violently until well past midnight.

He was beginning to doze when he noticed that her trembling had ceased. Pulling back, he looked down into her face. In the cold moonlight it was no longer flushed. Instead, it was a ghostly white. Reaching up with one hand, she touched his cheek.

"Good-bye, Skye," she told him. "I hope you find hombre you seek."

"Good-bye, Topaz," he told her, holding her frail hand against his cheek, the awful chill of it reaching into his soul.

Her eyes closed and her head sagged to one side, the fire within her finally quenched. Fargo stood up and looked down at Topaz for a long moment, unashamed tears coursing down his cheek. In solemn salute he touched his hat brim to her.

She had been one hell of a woman, and he would not soon forget her.

The next morning he left Topaz wrapped in her blanket, tucked into a hidden ledge high in the rocks to keep out the coyotes and wolves. Then he followed the canyon she had pointed out to him. By noon he reached a river. Turning upstream, he followed it until nightfall, then camped.

He built a fire and roasted his meager meal—a

scrawny jackrabbit he had shot from his saddle—then took his sleeping bag into the rocks above the fire's glowing embers. He knew the Apaches must still be on his trail, determined to avenge the death of Teenaro. Even if they found Topaz's body, it would not satisfy them. They could read sign the way a preacher could read scripture, and from the tracks Fargo must have left, the Apaches would be certain he had been Topaz's accomplice from the beginning. And they would not be wrong. From the moment Fargo took after Topaz, he knew she intended to kill Teenaro—and his intent had been to help her do so.

A little after dawn the next day, Fargo was saddling the pinto when he heard the clink of iron against stone. He turned to see an old prospector riding out from behind a boulder on the other side of the narrow stream less than twenty yards away, two heavily laden pack mules strung out behind him. As Fargo watched, the fellow nudged his mount into the swift water, his two mules following after him.

The old man held a shotgun in his hand, the twin bores yawning dangerously in Fargo's direction. Noting the gnarled finger tucked about the triggers, Fargo realized the weapon would go off if the horse stumbled in the swift stream or the prospector lost his balance. But the old man looked like a pretty good rider, despite his age.

He was short and round-shouldered, with a gut that flowed out over his gun belt. His face was raw from the sun except where a short white stubble of beard protected it. As he gained the bank, his shrewd, cautious eyes did not waver.

"Put down that shotgun, friend," Fargo told him. "You don't need it with me."

"Name's Clampett, Bud Clampett," the old man drawled. "Maybe I don't need this here Greener with you, but them Apaches on yer tail ain't no friends of mine."

"Apaches? How far back?"

"Last night they made camp about five miles downstream," he told Fargo, dropping his shotgun into his scabbard. "I figure they's a mite closer by now."

"My name's Skye Fargo," Fargo replied. "Thanks for the warning. Mind telling me what you're doing in these here mountains? You don't look like a rattlesnake or a scorpion."

The old man chuckled. "Been prospectin' in these here mountains for more'n fifteen years now."

"Any luck?"

"Don't look like it, does it? But I guess by now it don't matter I ain't found nothin'. This here sunblasted corner of Hades is my home. I know it almost as good as the Apaches. I don't mind them devils too much, but yer a white man, so maybe you better come with me."

"Lead on," Fargo replied, "and much obliged."

Fargo mounted up. The old man turned his mount around, rode back out onto the water, and continued upstream, the swift icy water lapping the horses' bellies. About three miles farther on, in the shade of a towering cliff, Clampett halted in a shallow pool and tied pieces of hide around the shoes of his horse and mules. Fargo did the same to his pinto.

About a quarter of a mile farther on, Clampett led Fargo slowly, carefully, out onto a stretch of caprock, the hide-covered shoes of their mounts leaving no trace on its smooth surface. They followed the caprock deep into a stand of white pine, then left it. Sending Fargo ahead through the timber, Clampett remained behind to cover their tracks by smoothing out the pine needles with a branch he dragged behind him. When Fargo reached a gravel bed Clampett had told him lay ahead, he pulled up and waited for the old man to overtake him.

They followed the gravel until it ran out, then followed another streambed until close to sundown. Then Clampett led Fargo to the rim of the canyon they had been following. Before the last rays of the sun faded from the sky, Fargo saw ahead of him the old man's shack, built against the side of a cliff, well in under a beetling overhang of rock, invisible until a few seconds before.

Dismounting, Clampett led his horse and mules toward a weathered shed that served as a barn. Behind the shed and the shack loomed a sheer cliff wall, the lower portion dark with moisture as a steady stream of water issued from a long fissure above. At the foot of the cliff gleamed a large pool of water.

"Tend to yore hoss while I tend to my animals," Clampett told Fargo. "Then we'll set a spell before supper. You must be plumb wore out."

Fargo nodded and followed the old man toward the shed, wondering why in hell Clampett wasn't worn out too.

Clampett swung the jug onto his right shoulder and took a healthy swallow. Wiping his mouth with the back of his hand, he passed the jug across the table to

Fargo. "I knowed it. First time I laid eyes on you, I said to myself, He's come for that silver."

"Not the silver," Fargo said, taking the jug. "The man in charge of the mule train, Federico Silva."

"You mean you don't want that silver if'n you can get it?"

"I didn't say that."

"You damn right you didn't."

"If you'd show me the way to Chimney Rock, I'd be much obliged."

"Why do you want to go there?"

Fargo told the old man of his encounter with John Carswell and his sons and what Tom had blurted, that the attack on the mule train had occurred near that rock.

Clampett nodded. "Tom was tellin' the truth, despite hisself. Hell, he was there—along with his pa and the rest of his clan."

Fargo sat back in his chair, astonished at Clampett's words. "Hold it right there, Clampett. You mean you saw them?"

"I was mebbe a mile away when I heard the shooting. By the time I got to Chimney Rock, the Indians was gone. Clampett and his clan must've ridden up and drove them off, from what I could see."

"Did you show yourself?" Fargo asked.

"You think I'm crazy? I kept myself hid. Didn't see no reason why I should tangle with them four rattlesnakes."

"Then you didn't see the Indians attack?"

"Nope. But I sure as hell heard them." Clampett snatched up the jug and took another swallow, belching loudly after he put it down.

"Them Indians, were they Apaches?"

Clampett shook his head emphatically. "Hell, no. They weren't no Apaches. They was Papagos!"

"I thought this land belongs to the Apache."

"Oh, they'd like you to think it does. But the Papagos, they's a good fightin' Indian, and they don't hesitate to track through Apache land. There's a whole passel of 'em beyond the Superstitions—and they got themselves a nice ripe valley, I hear tell."

"You never been there?"

"This here's my neck of the woods."

Fargo smiled at the old man affectionately. Clampett could probably have fixed himself a pretty snug cabin in a corner of hell, if the devil would allow it.

"So you think it was Papagos that attacked that train."

"That's what I said."

"You sure?"

"Don't I know an Apache from a Papago?" Clampett got up and stalked over to an Indian quiver leaning in a corner. He brought it over to the table and placed it down in front of Fargo. "Look there," he said, taking from it a couple of arrows. "These here is Apache arrows. See them small black shafts? And them markin's? Now look here—" He took from the quiver three longer, lighter arrows. "These here longer ones are Papago arrows. I found them sticking out of the mules and the two mule skinners when I went back a couple of days later."

"And you found no silver?"

"No silver, but I saw tracks of two mules and a mounted rider, heading off down a side canyon farther down."

"You mean the Indians must've missed him?"

"Yep." He grinned. "And so did the Carswells."

"How do you figure that?"

"Simple, if you can read sign. That feller wasn't with the mule train when the Papagos attacked. He was watchin' the whole thing from a safe spot farther down the canyon."

"You got any explanation for that?"

Clampett smiled. "Pretty clear, ain't it? That feller knowed ahead of time when and where them Indians was goin' to attack the mule train."

Fargo considered that for a moment, then nodded his agreement. It made good sense. "And something else is clear, too."

"What's that?"

"The Carswells knew."

The old man frowned. "Guess maybe they did, at that."

"Do me a favor."

"Sure."

"Take me to that spot tomorrow."

"I guess there won't be no harm in that." Clampett passed the jug back to Fargo. "Drink up. It'll freshen yore gums and liven up yore liver. And you'll sleep like a babe."

That night Fargo slept like a babe.

Riding past Chimney Rock the next morning with Clampett, Fargo was impressed. Less than two miles from Clampett's canyon, the formation reared high into the sky, resembling, as its name indicated, the titanic remnants of a chimney, the house it could have warmed scoured away by a ceaseless onslaught of hot, wind-driven sand.

Not long after, they rounded a bend and Fargo caught sight of an odd assortment of shapes and what looked like patches of dust-laden shrubbery scattered across the floor of the canyon.

"Here you be," Clampett said.

Fargo nodded. They had reached the spot where the mule team had been attacked.

The odd shapes were what was left of broken, looted wagons and torn-open packs; the dust-covered shrubbery were really the rib cages of two mule skinners and three mules struck down in the act of flight. Fargo reined up beside a looted wagon and dismounted. The bones were picked clean, and what clothing remained on the skeletal remains of the two mule skinners hung in dust-laden tatters from bones and rib cages.

"Here," said Clampett, reaching down and pulling an arrow from between a mule's rib cage.

Fargo took the arrow.

"You see the length of it? And the featherin'? Them's Papago arrows."

Fargo nodded and flung it away. Despite the searing sun overhead, he felt a momentary chill as he looked around this field of death, at how little the vultures had left of the mule skinners and their mules.

"Where were those tracks you mentioned?" Fargo asked Clampett. "The ones left by that mounted rider and the two mules farther up the canyon?"

"I'll show you."

They mounted up, and the old man led Fargo back to a fold in the canyon wall, about a quarter of a mile back. Dismounting, Clampett pointed to the ground. Squinting in the blazing sun, Fargo found himself able to make out the faint pattern of horse's hooves. There was very little to go on, however. The wind had almost completely filled the tracks with sand.

They led straight across the canyon and disappeared into a narrow side canyon on the other side.

"Where's that other canyon lead?" Fargo asked.

"To the Devil's Kitchen. If yer thinking of followin' them tracks, forget it."

"Why?"

"Even the Apaches steer clear of there. For maybe ten, fifteen miles that land's a home for rattlers and scorpions—and not much else. No one who rode into there has ever returned."

"Someone has, Clampett."

"Who?

"That fellow who came back to tell about all them rattlers and scorpions."

"Fargo," you'd be plumb loco to go in there. This feller yer after, the one who took the silver, he's a dead man now."

"I'm still going after him."

Clampett shrugged in weary resignation. "Then ride on back to my cabin first. I'll give you provisions and fill up some water bags fer you. You can rest up fer a couple of days, at least. You don't have to go rushin' in there right now."

"Maybe not. If you don't mind the company. Much obliged."

Clampett grinned. "Hell, no. I don't mind. A man gets a mite lonely out here."

Swinging into his saddle, Clampett pulled his mount

around and rode out into the middle of the canyon. Fargo had mounted up and was pulling his pinto around to follow when a rifle shot rang out and Clampett slipped sideways off his horse. Grabbing his Sharps from his scabbard, Fargo spurred out to see to Clampett, glancing down the canyon at the same time. Four horsemen were galloping toward him through the wavering curtain of heat.

In the lead was John Carswell, his three sons strung out behind him.

4

Leaping off the pinto beside Clampett's crumpled body, Fargo flung up the Sharps and squeezed off a round. Carswell's horse caught the slug in its brain. There was an explosion of blood and bone, and the horse went down so fast Carswell was flung over its head. He slammed to the hard ground and lay on his back for a second, dazed. Behind him his sons began firing.

Swiftly reloading, Fargo returned their fire. With a starled cry Seth spun off his horse, landing on his back. Tom and Billy Joe flung themselves from their mounts and dashed headlong for cover, while Carswell hauled Seth to his feet and flung him after his two craven sons.

Fargo draped the wounded Clampett over his pinto's neck, grabbed the reins of Clampett's horse, remounted, and galloped all the way across the canyon into the smaller side canyon, following Silva's tracks. He reached the safety of the canyon just as a bullet whined off a rock slab inches above his head.

Dismounting, Fargo ducked back to the canyon's mouth and returned Carswell's fire, aiming the Sharps at the rocks above and behind the spot where he and his three sons were crouching. Reloading with metronomic speed, he poured a steady fusillade at them. He heard their sudden cries of dismay as the slugs ricocheted around them like a swarm of angry hornets, and saw them scramble out of the rocks and race down the canyon.

Leaning his Sharps against a boulder, Fargo lifted the old prospector off the pony.

"Clampett," Fargo whispered, resting him down on the ground as gently as possible.

Clampett didn't answer. His mouth was slack, his eyes lusterless. Ripping off Clampett's shirt and turning him over, Fargo saw a hole the size of his fist. Carswell's round had shattered the prospector's spine, then ranged up into his lungs and heart, killing him instantly. The old prospector would get lonely no more.

Fargo returned to the side canyon's entrance. "Carswell!"

"Throw down your weapon, Fargo," Big John cried. "We got you dead to rights."

"You just killed an innocent man. You'll pay for that. With your life. And that's a promise!"

For response, Carswell lifted himself high enough to send a round at Fargo. It whined harmlessly off a rock above him. Fargo sent a few quick rounds back at Carswell, then began peppering the ground in front of the three horses his sons had abandoned in the middle of the canyon. As the geysers of sand exploded at their feet, the horses reared in terror, wheeled, and stampeded down the canyon. Tom and Billy Joe raced out from the rocks to try to stop them, but the horses veered sharply and kept going.

In a moment they were out of sight.

Darting back to his pinto, Fargo stepped into his saddle and rode off down the narrow canyon, pulling Clampett's horse after him. As he rode, he kept his eyes on the faint trail left by Federico Silva. Behind him, he knew, Carswell and his three sons had a long walk ahead of them. They would be lucky if they made it out of these mountains alive.

Fargo hoped they did. He wanted very much to keep his promise to Carswell.

After a few miles the canyon widened until he was riding over a level, barren flat containing little vegetation and no sign of water. He was forced to detour constantly around massive boulders and monolithic slabs of black, gleaming basalt, protruding from the ground like the heads of titanic lances. The canyon walls closed in on him again as he rode between walls of flaming sandstone that loomed so high they shut out the sky's single, blazing eye.

Squinting in the satanic heat, his bandanna pulled up over his face to protect himself from the stinging, wind-driven sand, Fargo followed what remained of Silva's trail.

The wagon tracks eventually led into a narrow arroyo littered with sharp boulders, forcing Fargo to slow the pinto to a walk as he picked his way along. At last the arroyo's walls fell away and the trail ahead of him gave way to a slanting rock slope. Fargo kept on down the slope, skirting more boulders, then picked his way across a wide, gravel-filled wash until once again—still following Silva's trail—he found himself moving along a winding, sheer-walled draw cut through red sandstone.

Relieved to be free of the sun's oppressive heat, he continued until he came to a small pool gleaming in the shadow of a towering rock wall. It was not yet noon, but he decided to make camp. Pulling the saddles off both animals, he refilled his canteens and was looking for a place to rest his weary bones when he heard the pinto's sharp, terrified whinny behind him. Spinning about, he saw both horses rearing almost straight up, their forelegs kicking out frantically, while two sidewinders slithered out of the patch of sunlight at their feet and vanished into the shadows of a boulder.

Whether or not the rattlers had succeeded in sinking their fangs into the horses' hooves made no difference. The damage had already been done. Fargo reached out frantically to grab the pinto's head, but the pony twisted away. Fargo caught a glimpse of dilated nostrils and wide, staring eyes as the Ovaro wheeled and galloped back up the draw, Clampett's horse following close behind.

Fargo chased after the horses until he could run no farther and slumped to the ground, exhausted. When he got his wind back, he returned to the pool, slumped down in the cool shadows beside it, his head back against the wall.

Out of the corner of his eye he caught a slight movement. Turning his head, he glanced down at the spot where the rock wall met the trail. The centuries of flash flooding that had sliced this arroyo out of solid rock had cut into the bottom of the rock wall as well, scouring out a cool, damp passageway—a refuge from the terrible sun.

The tail of a rattler, its rattles not yet quivering, was poking out from under the cliff wall less than two feet from him. Turning his head slightly and bending forward, Fargo peered into the shadows and saw what appeared to be a great opened can of worms—a nest of rattlers. Glancing farther along the base of the wall, his eyes caught still more movement and for the first time Fargo became aware of the dim buzzing of countless rattlers up and down the arroyo.

He leaned back against the wall, cold sweat standing out on his forehead. He had made camp in a snake-infested hellhole, a refuge from the midday heat that belonged, not to him, but to the sidewinder.

Picking up his hat, he inspected it nervously before putting it back on his head. Then he lugged his gear slowly and quietly out into the middle of the arroyo, where patches of sunlight seared the ground. Then he went back for the three canteens. His only safety, he knew now, lay in keeping himself in the blazing sunshine; the cooler, shady spots belonged to the sidewinders.

He couldn't stay where he was. Beyond the arroyo a draw yawned, slanting down into another, deeper canyon, the floor of which was bright with sunlight. Fargo had no choice but to make for it. As soon as this place cooled off, the snakes would leave their midday refuge to forage. Slinging the canteens over one shoulder, his bedroll over the other, Fargo started down the draw, heading for the lower canyon. He hated to leave his saddle, but promised himself he could return for it when he came back for his pinto.

He followed the draw until it opened into a fissure, a twisting rent in the ground that cut down through the layered red rock toward the canyon below. The draw offered a way down, but it wouldn't be easy. Tossing his bedroll ahead of him to the canyon below, he worked his way down the steep, gravelly trail, watching carefully to see that he did not place a foot close to any nesting rattlers or reach his hand in under a shady rock to arouse a scorpion's sudden fury. By this time it had occurred to him to heed Clampett's warning to expect scorpions as well as sidewinders. This was land only sidewinders and scorpions could love.

He dropped rapidly, red dirt and loose rock showering down upon his shoulders, raining on his hat brim, until at last the cut opened out onto a broad, sloping ledge that left him at least twenty feet above the canyon floor. He walked to the end of the ledge and looked over. The stream that cut through the canyon had left a pool under him, and the wall facing that curving sweep of water had been undercut deeply, forming a great, open-faced cavern. Great slabs of red-veined rock had peeled away from the wall and fallen into the pool.

It was not much of a jump. He tossed his hat and his canteens down onto the sand surrounding the pool, then exmained the boulder-pocked surface of the water carefully, aware that if he came down on one of those chunks of stone, he could break a leg—or worse. Moving down the ledge, he picked his spot carefully and grabbed hold of a protruding rock held in place by the gnarled roots of a piñon. Very carefully, he lowered himself over the ledge until he was hanging full length. He looked down between his feet. There was only one boulder in sight, which meant he would have to kick outward before letting go.

He glanced back up at the ledge. A scorpion, its hooked stinger poised to strike, was emerging rapidly from under the roots of the piñón, obviously furious at the giant whose hands were tugging on the rock under its apartment.

Fargo didn't bother to glance down a second time. Kicking out as far as he could go, he let go. He hit the water feet-first and knew he had missed the boulder. The water closed momentarily over his head. Plunging blindly forward and blowing furiously, he charged out of the pool and flung himself down on the rim of sand surrounding it. Glancing up at the ledge, he shook his head wearily, mightily relieved to have escaped that scorpion. He put his hand down onto a rock to push himself upright. The rock moved under his weight and he felt something tickling the back of his hand. Glancing down, he saw a scorpion clinging to it.

Jumping up, Fargo waved his hand wildly. The scorpion struck the rock wall at his back, then rebounded onto him. He flung himself about and started beating at his clothes. His feet dislodged a few boulders resting against the rock wall and a rattler appeared and began to reach up for him, its tongue flickering, its dry rattle filling the air with its warning.

Fargo turned about and ran from the canyon wall and hurried across the sand ringing the pool to the spot where he had thrown his hat and the canteens. When he reached down for them, he found his hair was standing on end, his mind cold with fear—the kind of instinctive, primordial terror that threatened to shatter his self-control.

Gathering up the canteens, Fargo slapped his hat back on, then hoisted the bedroll onto his shoulders. Glancing back, he shuddered. Usually a scorpion's bite was no more severe than that of a bee or a wasp. But one glance had told him that this last one clinging to his hand was a deadly buthid scorpion, native not only to Arizona but also to the land around Sonora in Mexico. It injected a poison lethal enough to kill a child—or even a grown man if he was bitten high enough on the neck. Years before, Fargo had witnessed the death of an Indian boy who had suffered such a bite. Even now Fargo could recall clearly the pitiful, labored breathing of the dying child, the maddening restlessness, the painful shrieks, and the constant flow of saliva.

Turning back around, Fargo set off toward the distant peaks ringing this land of sun-scorched sand and rock. Only on the other side of that range would he be safe.

Three days later, Fargo left his bedroll behind.

It was close to noon. He had been walking in the sun since that morning. Ahead of him loomed a low outcropping of rocks. They offered blessed shade. When he reached the rocks, he threw himself down onto the ground and rested his head back onto his bedroll, too weary to check the area first for rattlers or scorpions.

After a moment or two, his natural caution regained the upper hand and he sat up to look around, but he found it difficult to focus his eyes. He did not try to wipe off the red dust that caked his roasted face. To his swollen tongue, his lips felt like a series of scabs as they cracked open, scabbed, then cracked again. He had had to conserve what water remained in one of his canteens as the fierce sun had drawn nearly all the moisture from his body. Two days before he had shot a jackrabbit with his Colt and eaten it raw. The memory of that succulent feast still warmed him.

He allowed himself a taste of water from his canteen, the neck searing his lips, then dropped off. The sun awoke him. It was shining full in his face. He stirred himself, then got to his feet. He was about to reach down for his bedroll, then realized it was too much for him to carry any farther. Taking one last glimpse of it, he flung his clinking canteens over his shoulder and started up again, his Sharps in his right hand.

By this time there were no more wheel tracks in the dust, no hoofprints etched in the sand for him to follow. All he could do now was keep on going, heading due west into the blazing eye of the sun until he reached those low peaks sitting on the horizon. Beyond that dark, jagged rim, he prayed, lay a kinder, less deadly land. . . .

Fargo shook the canteen. Nothing. He tossed it down the slope and watched it bounce to the bottom of the draw, coming to rest noisily in the midst of hog-sized boulders. He had reached the rocky uplands he had been trudging toward, but all he had found was a maze of twisting canyons and rocky draws.

And no water.

His tongue was a raw, swollen piece of punishment by this time, moistureless and painful. His lips had cracked and remained open. Every muscle, every sinew, every creaking joint in his massive frame, seemed to cry out for water.

Fargo trudged on. A jackrabbit broke from a patch of brush under a cliff. Fargo brought up his Sharps and fired. As the bullet shattered a rock beside it, the rabbit vanished into some brush. Fargo took a deep breath to calm himself, then dropped a fresh linen cartridge into the Sharps and slammed up the trigger guard.

The next time, he promised himself, he would not miss.

Soon the canyon began to wind back upon itself, the walls closing in ominously. The towering, sheer walls blocked out the sky on occasion. It was much cooler in the shade of the canyon's walls, but despite his weariness, he was careful where he put his feet down. As he knew from experience, he would not be the only living thing in this terrible land seeking refuge from that hellish sun.

Turning a corner, the Trailsman saw, cut out of the rock wall ahead of him, a narrow fissure just wide enough to admit a grown man. Reaching it, he peered into the passageway. A cool wind seemed to blow from it. Without hesitation, he squeezed into it and kept going until he found himself looking down at a circular depression in the sand. At the very bottom he glimpsed a patch of dark sand.

He had found a hole that until recently had held water! And there was a good chance there would be some water left in the center, below the damp sand.

Scrambling into the empty water hole, Fargo went down on his knees and began clawing through the sand. He had dug a hole almost a foot deep when he let out a sudden cry and yanked his hand back. Jumping to his feet, he slapped at his right hand with his left, dislodging a scorpion clinging with its pincers to his forefinger. As the scorpion struck the ground and began to scurry off, Fargo drew his Colt and emptied it at the insect. His last bullet caught the scorpion, splattering it to bits.

Only then did Fargo glance at the back of his gun hand.

He knew he had not been stung. If he had, he would already have felt the effects of the paralyzing venom. But a moment longer and the stinger on the scorpion's tail would have plunged home.

Taking a deep breath, Fargo looked around. There was no water left in the sand, he realized, even if he were to dig clear to China. Sheer rock walls enclosed him on all sides. Catching sight of one crevice, the sides of which seemed to have been worn particularly smooth, he realized it was down through this chute in the rocks that the water must have cascaded, turning this large, natural bowl into a churning water hole. Had Fargo come a week or so earlier, he realized, he would have found some brackish water still left in it.

Moving closer to the wall, Fargo glanced up at the crevice and found himself looking up into the wide, dead eyes of Federico Silva. Less than five feet above him, Silva's body was caught between two shoulders of rock, both of his bony, parchmentlike hands reaching down for the water he craved. It was clear what had happened.

Silva must have caught from above the glint of

water in the pool below and had started to climb down through the rock fracture. But in his haste he had slipped and fallen, jamming himself between those two rocky projections. His death must have been long and terrible as he died within sight of the water beckoning to him just beyond his reach.

Fargo felt a chill fall over him as he gazed up at the hapless fellow. He was not, after all, the man Fargo sought. He was Federico Silva, all right, but now that Fargo could see him closer, he realized this was not one of the four men he had glimpsed boiling out of the Express office that day so many long years before.

Wearily, Fargo struggled back through the narrow fissure.

A day later Fargo still had not found water. And he was no longer thinking clearly as he stumbled across a sun-baked flat. Directly ahead of him loomed the outer rim of the Superstition Mountains, their flanks cool and inviting, less than a day away now. They might as well have been on the surface of the moon. Fargo had stretched himself to the limit, then kept on past that point. But he was only made of flesh and blood.

He stumbled once, twice, then sprawled awkwardly forward onto the blistering ground. Muttering, he pushed himself erect and tried to get up. But his limbs had lost all power to answer his commands and he collapsed a second time. He was now reduced to crawling, and even that with difficulty. He tried it for a while and gave up on it, disgusted with himself, and found with some surprise that he was lying on his back, staring up at the sun.

He closed his eyes and rolled over slowly. Pulling

in his arms, he made one last, determined effort to push himself to his feet. But the best he could manage was to sit up. Dazedly, he blinked into the distance, staring at the cool mountain ramparts shimmering in the heat.

The sun was pressing down on the back of his neck like a branding iron. Reaching his hand up, he realized he had lost his hat. He turned his head and saw it lying on the ground a good distance behind him, his Sharps gleaming alongside it. Concentrating mightily, he turned himself around and began to crawl toward the hat.

When he got close enough, he reached for it, but the hat, lying on its crown, rolled away when his unsteady hand brushed the rim. A shadow passed over him. He glanced up and saw the broad spread of a vulture's wing as the bird circled in a searing updraft less than ten feet above him. A second bird was drifting down toward him as well. Fargo looked away from the two birds and reached out frantically for his hat.

Before his fingers touched the brim, he felt the vulture's talons closing upon his blistered neck. His rasping cry of dismay and horror echoed futilely in the vast amphitheater of sun and rock. A second shadow fell over him as the other buzzard joined the first.

Fargo turned to beat feebly, futilely, at the foul bird's talons, then fell away into a blessed, cooling darkness. . . .

5

A girl's cool hand was resting on Fargo's brow.

Opening his eyes, he stared up at her. She was beautiful. This had to be some kind of dream.

"Don't tell me," he said. "Let me tell you."

"I'm listening," the girl replied, her voice low, a hint of laughter in it. "Go ahead and tell me."

"I've died and gone to heaven."

"Close, but no cigar." The girl laughed, gently pressing a cooling wet compress down onto his brow. "You're in my bedroom."

"This is your place?"

"Yes."

"And where would that be?"

"In a Papago village on the other side of the Superstition Mountains."

She reached back to a small wicker stand by the cot, picked up a water jug, and filled a cup with water. Beads of moisture were sitting on the outside of the jug, and the sound of the water being poured into the cup was music to his ears. He sat up.

"Here," the girl said, handing him the cup and taking the compress from him. "But do drink it slowly."

Nodding, he sipped the water slowly, his scabbed lips making this difficult. When he had emptied the cup, she asked if he wanted more. He nodded and watched her fill it again.

She looked to be about twenty-two years old and was dressed in a light-blue homespun cotton blouse and a long cotton skirt banded with yellow and red stripes.

"What's your name?" he asked when he finished the second cup.

"Carlotta," she replied.

"I'm Fargo, Skye Fargo," he told her, sipping the water. "At least that's the handle I used when I was back on earth."

"Then it is still your name, I assure you."

A tall, powerful Indian, bare to the waist and wearing buckskin leggings, entered the bedroom and came to a halt beside Carlotta. Like an Apache, he kept his long hair in place with a red headband, but he was taller than most Apaches, his face narrower, his nose more prominent.

"How are you, stranger?" the Indian asked.

"His name's Fargo, Dano," Carlotta told the Indian.

"I'm okay, thanks," Fargo replied.

The Indian smiled, his teeth brilliant in his dark face. "You're lucky. We found you just in time."

"You led us all a merry chase," Carlotta explained.

"I don't understand—"

"There'll be time for explanations later," Carlotta

told him. "For now, you just stay quiet and rest awhile longer while I see to your food. Are you hungry?"

The question opened a void in the cavern beneath his ribs. He nodded quickly. "I reckon maybe you could say that."

Carlotta and Dano left.

Fargo filled the cup for himself, sipped about half the cup, then placed it down beside the sweating water jug. Then he lay back down, content just to be able to glance over at the jug of water every now and then.

Closing his eyes, he let his thoughts drift back as he tried to get his bearings. Memories of his last days in the mountains returned to him in vague, tantalizing snatches . . . Indians lifting him, their dark faces peering impassively down into his . . . a rocking motion and a sense of the sky whirling by above him as the sound of hooves clopped steadily over rocky ground . . . the presence of Carlotta hovering anxiously over him, dabbing at his scorched face with cooling compresses, at his raw lips with soothing unguents.

At the end of it came a descent into cool, sunless darkness, broken only occasionally by the sound of Carlotta's musical voice . . . the gentle buzz of voices . . . the pad of moccasined feet passing his window . . .

Carlotta entered with an Indian woman by her side. Both were carrying food. Carlotta had a stack of wheatcakes on a large earthen platter, while the Indian woman was carrying a steaming bowl of broth with what looked like chunks of mutton and slices of wild onion swimming in it. Carlotta put her plate of wheatcakes down on the wicker stand next to the water jug; the Indian woman placed her bowl beside it.

Setting down a large cup filled with honey beside the wheatcakes, Carlotta said, "I am sorry, but we have no coffee."

"Who's complaining?"

She turned then and spoke to the Indian woman in a dialect Fargo recognized as related to the Yaqui Indians to the south. The woman nodded, then left, while Carlotta made herself comfortable on a thick blanket she folded on the floor, crossing her legs and watching him intently, her dark, slender arms resting in the bowl her skirt made.

There was a sadness about her face, a melancholy emphasized by her high cheekbones and the lines about her eyes, which seemed to peer too deeply and see too far. At times they were a clear, soft green. At other times they were dark, as they were at this moment. Her forehead was high, almost lofty, her luxuriant dark hair swept back, a blue cotton band keeping it off her face.

"The soup will get cold," she chided him softly.

Fargo looked away from her quickly and set to work on his meal. He found the wheatcakes delicious. And the thick, boldly seasoned soup sent warmth and strength radiating out from his stomach, while the chunks of mutton were as soft and sweet as candy.

When he had had his fill, he leaned back and smiled down at Carlotta, fighting back a belch.

"Feel better?" she asked, getting to her feet.

"Much better. Thanks."

As if by magic the Indian woman entered, set down

a fresh jug of water, and cleared away the empty dishes.

"It is good to see a hungry man eat," Carlotta said, sitting on the edge of his cot.

"It feels good to eat when you're hungry."

"I can imagine. You were in terrible shape when we found you."

He nodded. "I do remember staring up at a dead man wedged into a rock cleft. After that, it gets pretty hazy. Last thing I knew I was fighting off vultures."

"Are you calling me a vulture?" she laughed.

"Was that you?"

"As a matter of fact, I did reach your side first and you did struggle with me feebly, before passing out."

"You mind telling me what you were doing in that hellhole?"

"Following your tracks. As I said before, you led us a merry chase."

Fargo frowned. "But why in blazes were you chasing me?"

"That will come later," she said gently, peering intently at him. "Tell me, Fargo, aren't you tired?"

Fargo frowned. As a matter of fact, he was. Very tired. His limbs were turning to lead and his eyelids sat on his eyes like anvils. "Carlotta," he managed, "did you put something in that broth?"

She smiled. "How did you guess? It won't hurt you. It is an herb native to this valley. You'll sleep well now, I promise."

She moved close and pushed him back gently onto the cot. As he drifted off, he felt Carlotta's swift, cool hands pulling the blanket up over his naked shoulders.

*   *   *

A familiar whicker coming from just outside his window aroused him the next morning. He sat up quickly and peered out. His Ovaro was standing in full view, looking as fit as a fiddle. As soon as the handsome black-and-white Ovaro caught sight of Fargo's face in the window, he whickered a second time and began bobbing his head. Damned if the horse wasn't trying to apologize for running out on him.

Flinging off the blanket Carlotta had thrown over him, Fargo wrapped it about his naked figure and padded on bare feet out of the bedroom. With only a curt nod to the Indian woman working in the kitchen, he hurried outside.

Carlotta was standing beside the pony, laughing. "You see? I know how to awaken you."

Fargo took the pinto's halter and pulled him close. When he draped his arms over his neck, the pony whickered contentedly.

"He's in fine shape," said Carlotta.

"No sign of a bite? That hellhole was full of side-winders and scorpions."

"Nothing, I assure you. We checked."

Fargo patted the pinto affectionately on the neck. "Where'd you find him?"

"We caught him and another horse soon after we began tracking you. Then we found your saddle. Once we realized you were on foot, we became concerned."

"Hell, Carlotta, you didn't know me from a gopher hole. And I never laid eyes on you before I woke up yesterday. So how come you were concerned about me?"

"My, aren't you suspicious!"

"You haven't answered me."

Carlotta shrugged. "We saw you take on John Carswell and his boys."

Dano strode up then and halted beside Carlotta, his eyes sweeping enviously over the handsome animal.

Fargo nodded his morning greeting to the Indian, then looked back at Carlotta. "Now, just why in blazes should my taking on Big John make any difference to you?"

Dano spoke up then. "You are first white man who dare tangle with him."

"You see, Skye," said Carlotta, "we are having trouble with Carswell."

"What kind of trouble?"

"Bad trouble. He wants this valley."

"And you think my gun will come in handy?"

"And your rifle," said Dano. "It is very powerful. It has long reach."

"It's a Sharps. It should have."

Carlotta stepped back to look him over. Then, smiling, she shook her head. "Skye, I hope you aren't planning to go around in that blanket all day."

"Have you a better idea?"

"I most certainly have. Your clothes are all washed and dried. Let me bring them in to you."

Fargo nodded and started back to Carlotta's adobe hut, Dano leading the pinto off. At the doorway, Fargo turned to get one more glimpse of the mount he thought he'd never see again. Beyond the adobe village a green meadowland extended as far as the mountain peaks that rimmed this pleasant valley, and it was toward that cool splash of green that Dano was leading the lucky pinto.

Content, Fargo turned and entered the adobe house.

A moment later, Carlotta arrived with his clean buckskins and the rest of his clothing. Fargo began to dress, expecting Carlotta to leave the bedroom. But she did nothing of the sort, watching him casually as he stepped out of his blanket stark-naked and pulled on his underdrawers and then his tight buckskin pants. Her presence had an effect on a sensitive portion of his anatomy that should have made her at least turn away. Instead, her dark eyes seemed to grow just a mite darker, while something akin to an excited blush suffused her face.

As he was pulling on his boots, the Indian woman arrived with his breakfast. More wheatcakes and honey, and since there was no coffee, a strong tequilalike drink that warmed his insides clear down to his big toe.

"Ready?" Carlotta asked after he had finished his meal.

"For what?"

"I want to show you our settlement so you'll understand about this trouble we're having with Carswell."

Fargo walked over to the corner of the room where his gun belt had been piled alongside his Sharps rifle and bedroll. As he reached down for the gun belt, Carlotta said, "You won't need that, Skye. Not here in this valley."

With a shrug, Fargo straightened and buckled on his gun belt. "I'd be walking lopsided," he told her, "without this here iron to balance me."

"Suit yourself."

Checking the Colt's load, Fargo dropped the weapon back into his holster. "Okay," he said, "lead on."

The village impressed Fargo. It was clean and neatly

laid out, with none of the casual disorder that characterized so many Indian encampments. Carlotta's was the only adobe building in the village.

The Papagos lived in dome-shaped brush huts, far neater in appearance than the somewhat similar Apache wickiups. Some of the larger brush huts were covered with brightly decorated blankets, while many were plastered neatly with adobe. The entire village sat on a flat baked white in the sun, so that the village looked like a neat arrangements of bright, overturned earthen bowls sitting in the sun to dry.

The Papago Indians themselves were handsome for the most part and went about dressed in ponchos and robes decorated with bright, colorful designs. The women seemed unable or unwilling to go anywhere unless they were carrying something on their backs attached to wooden frames. Others were busy weaving large, intricate baskets, while friendly burros wandered around like overgrown pets.

Behind the village loomed a high cliff, and glancing up at it, Fargo saw ladders leading up into great dark squares hollowed out of the cliff face. Squinting through the bright sunlight, he caught glimpses of Indians moving about high above him in the shadowed recesses.

"These Papagos are cliff dwellers?" Fargo asked Carlotta.

"No," Carlotta said, "but they are wise enough to use the cliff for storage and, if the time comes, for defense."

"Not a bad idea," Fargo said, peering up at what could easily become quite effective battlements. "It would take an army to dislodge anyone from those cliffs."

Soon they left the village behind and reached a low rise that looked away from the village, out over the valley. Carlotta halted and pointed to the green fields spread out below them. The individual fields seemed held together by what appeared to be an intricate, gleaming web of canals. Fargo realized at once what they were—irrigation ditches, similar to those he had once glimpsed in Utah.

"See those canals?" she asked.

Fargo nodded. "That's a pretty extensive bit of irrigation. Did these here Papagos build all them canals?"

"Not entirely," she said, leading him down the slope until they found themselves walking along a narrow, well-kept footpath running along one of the canals. "My father helped them to rebuild it."

"Your father?"

"He was an American—no, he came from America, but his youth he spent in Scotland." She frowned. "I remember him telling me about Scotland." She paused for a moment lost in thought.

"Go on," Fargo urged.

"Anyway, he lived in Texas for a while, then practiced medicine in Mexico City until he got into some trouble."

"What kind of trouble?"

"The kind I am sure you know all about, Skye," she said, glancing at him mischievously.

"Oh," he said. "Women."

"I knew you'd understand."

When they came to stone steps leading down toward the canal they had been following, Carlotta took his hand and led him down them until they had reached the last step, inches above the water. Then, after slipping off her moccasins, she helped him pull off his boots, and they both sat down and let their feet dangle in the water while Carlotta told Fargo about her father and the Papagos.

"With not one but two irate husbands on his trail, my father disguised himself as a priest and fled from Mexico City back across the border into the United States. When he came to this valley, he discarded his cassock and became again a doctor and healer, though this time the healer of a people."

"Healer of a people?"

"Yes. That was how he spoke of it. What he meant was he went to work repairing and rebuilding for the Papagos the ancient irrigation system he had discovered when he first entered the valley."

Fargo looked back at the canals and the fields they irrigated. He saw wheat as well as corn. In the midst of a desert, lush green. He looked back at Carlotta. "You mean these canals were already here?"

"No, not exactly. Not the way they are now, I mean. There were only traces of them. Most of the canals were just overgrown, weed-choked ditches then," she said. "The gates and sluices were gone completely. As irrigation canals, they were useless."

"Who set up the irrigation system in the first place, before they fell apart?"

"The First People—the Hohokam."

"The what?"

"The Hohokam."

"Sounds like a lot of hokum to me."

She frowned at him. "I do not think I know what you mean."

He laughed. "Go on. Tell me about the hokum."

"The Hohokam, Skye. They are the people who have gone away. The Wise Ones. Once they lived in this land for thousands of years, my father told me. They were a peaceful people. Grinders of meal and singers of songs, he called them. They built these miles of irrigation canals in the river valleys of this region. A tremendous undertaking," she said proudly, as if she herself had been a part of it, "not only in building the canals, but maintaining them so well that my father was able to make use of them once again for our people."

"I guess I'm impressed," Fargo said.

"You should be," she said. "I know of one network north of here that runs almost a hundred and fifty miles along the flanks of a single river. My father wanted my people to move our village to that spot before he died, but we decided to stay here in this valley, beside the mountains that have protected us for so long."

"Where does the water come from?"

"Springs. There are many underground springs all along this valley."

"So after your father fixed up this irrigation system for the Indians, he married your mother?"

"He married her before that, and he had to live in her mother's house. Maybe that is why he spent so much time in the fields working on the canals." She smiled. "That is what some people said."

"Could be," Fargo said. "What happened to your mother?"

"She died not long after my father's death."

"If he had to move in with your mother, that means the women run things around here, huh?"

"Almost," Carlotta replied, laughing. "After all, the women do most of the work—though, since Father, the men do help a lot in the fields."

"You mean he set a good example?"

"Yes," she said. "He worked very hard."

"I'll say it again. I'm impressed."

Fargo got up and pulled on his socks, then his boots. Watching him, she said, "There is something else I want to show you."

"I'm game."

Slipping on her moccasins, she led the way back up the steps and through a wheatfield, coming presently to a series of rolling hills, one of which commanded the entire valley. They were almost to its crest when Fargo saw the large adobe house, built in among a stand of immense cottonwoods.

Pulling up to gaze at it, Carlotta said, "I was born in that house."

"Pretty fancy, so far from civilization."

"It was enough to get my mother out of her people's hut. Wait until you see the inside. It has many rooms, upstairs and down, and a library filled with books. My people hold it sacred. They say the spirit of my father dwells within it still, watching over the valley he brought back to life."

They entered the adobe house. The first room Carlotta showed him was the library. It had a beamed ceiling and adobe walls, and shelf after shelf laden with books. In the center of the room was a large table and, sitting beside that, a portable blackboard with fresh chalk and a blackboard eraser in the tray.

Pausing beside the blackboard, Carlotta said, "This is where my father taught me, and where I have taught many of my people. With the money we got from his share of the wheat and corn he sold in Sonora, Mexico, he brought back these books, and much else besides."

She led Fargo from the library up a steep flight of stairs to the second floor. From the landing Fargo could see four rooms. Carlotta led him into the largest, one that looked out over the valley.

"This was my parents' room," she said. "It was here my father died. I have left it exactly as it was when he lived here."

Fargo looked around. It was not a cluttered room. The walls were hung with Papago blankets. The bed was large and covered with a very beautiful, magnificently designed Mexican blanket. There was a rolltop desk in one corner and above it several more shelves of books. Fargo went to the window. He could just make out the village through the cottonwoods.

Carlotta led him then to the next room.

"And this room was mine," she said, stepping in ahead of Fargo.

Fargo followed in after her and looked around.

"I was born in here," Carlotta explained softly, as if the ghost of her childhood still lived in the room. "I slept here until my parents died. Then I left and built my present house in the village, closer to my people."

"You built that adobe home yourself?"

"Dano and many others helped me."

Fargo looked around. Carlotta's room contained a dresser with a mirror attached, and on the dresser sat a comb-and-brush set. Along one wall stood a large, cedar freestanding closet, and through the half-opened door Fargo saw bright fabrics and the skirts of colorful dresses. The bed was large and canopied, painted white with gold trim in the French fashion. Over the canopy and the white, flowered coverlet, there should have been a thin patina of dust. But it was spotless.

He ran his fingers along the coverlet to make sure.

"A woman comes in every day," Carlotta explained, noting Fargo's action. "I told you. This is a very special place for my people."

"I can believe it."

"Someday I will take a husband and return here to live. And this will be the bedroom of my child."

"Sounds very nice."

With a deft movement, Carlotta flipped back the coverlet. Fargo looked at her in astonishment as she quickly shook out her dark hair, then lifted her blouse over her head. A second later her skirt swirled to the floor and she stood before him, naked, the dark splash of her pubic hair almost matching the sheen of the long dark tresses that now fell about her breasts. From head to toe, she was a deep, lustrous brown. Her breasts lifted high and firm, the nipples erect.

Without a word, she reached out to him. He stepped into her arms and kissed her. At first her lips were clumsy in their sudden, eager passion, but he took charge, and as she helped him peel out of his clothes, he bore her under him to the bed. The moment he was naked, he knelt astride her and began sucking her marvelous breasts, while he let his hand fall upon her pubis and began massaging gently her already moist mound. Then his lips worked their way down her belly, and even farther. She cried out in eagerness and began thrusting up wildly, her fingers digging into his hair.

"Oh, Skye," she whimpered.

His lips found their way back to hers. She opened her mouth eagerly and their tongues began clashing. She grabbed his erection and with almost brutal urgency guided him into her. As he sank deep, she gasped with pleasure. "Yes, Skye!" she muttered fiercely. "Oh, yes!"

He leaned back on his knees, grabbed a pillow, and thrust it under her buttocks, then went to work, slowly at first, bringing her along gently, but not too swiftly— then holding back for a while, teasing her, driving her almost to distraction, until at last he could no longer play the game and was forced to give himself over to his own pleasures.

He whaled away at her furiously, at times afraid he was hurting her, but she clung to him fiercely without complaint, grunting with each thrust, her head flipping from side to side. And by that time there was no turning back.

At last he felt her shuddering and bucking under him like a wild bronc as she began to climax. That set him off. He found himself roaring to his peak, laughing out loud, to come at last in a great, surging explosion. He flung his head back and roared in appreciation. . . .

As he rolled off Carlotta a moment later, still panting slightly, she looked at him with wide, wondering eyes.

"Do you always tease like that?" she wanted to know.

"When the mood strikes me."

"It was wonderful. We had so much *fun!*"

"Hell, Carlotta, that's what it's supposed to be, isn't it? Fun?"

"Oh, yes, but usually you white men—and your women, too, I am afraid—make it all such a solemn game."

"Now, how would you know that?"

"I have not lived in this valley all my life. My father sent me to St. Louis to a convent for my education. Though the convent sisters were very strict, I was able to learn much about the white women and their poor men. I was glad to get back here to this valley, I can tell you. Now, occasionally, I go on shopping trips to a little town not more than a day's journey from here, a place called Phoenix."

"I've been there."

"So you see, Skye, I am not an innocent."

He knew how dangerous it would be for him to say anything at that point. Instead, he smiled at her and ran one finger down her brow and over her nose. When he touched her lips, she grabbed his hand, stuck his finger into her mouth, and began to suck it, flicking it with her tongue as she did so.

It was amazing the effect it had on him.

She saw his growing erection with wide, delighted eyes and moved swiftly closer to him, her hand reaching down to fondle him. A few expert strokes and he was ready for her again. As he started to push her back down onto the bed, she shook her head.

"No," she told him fiercely. "Now it is my turn to tease you. I will ride you slow, Skye—so slow!"

Suiting action to words, she swung onto him, suspended herself over his quivering erection for a tantalizing moment, then lowered herself onto it with a mastery and a gentleness that delighted him. As she came to rest, she wriggled her behind just a little and settled in at least a couple of inches lower, so that her moist, flexing warmth had completely engulfed his shaft.

He leaned his head back then as she began to rock imperceptibly, the pace of her motion increasing only gradually. It was delicious. He felt as if he were riveted to her flesh as a slow fire began to build in his groin. She looked down at him as if from a great height, smiling happily. Giving him pleasure warmed her as much as it delighted him. Gradually the tempo increased, only to slow again and come almost to a complete halt. Then she would start up again. Each time she did this, she moved faster than the time before until he was in a fever of suspense.

"Don't stop, Carlotta," he told her, grabbing her waist and holding her down onto him. "Not this time!"

She nodded, rocking furiously. "I can't," she managed. "Not *now*."

Her face hardened into a grimace of pleasure as she flung her head back and closed her eyes. By then Fargo was lost himself in the fine frenzy of it. She was riding him wildly but with infinite skill. Each downward thrust of her body seemed to meld them into one complete, passionate entity. Yet, whenever she rose along his shaft, he felt again the terror of losing her until once more he had met her thrust and plowed his engorged shaft deep within her fiery muff.

Her climax came almost before he was aware of it. He heard her gasping shriek, and then she was leaning forward onto him, her large, incandescent breasts slamming into his face, her fists beating him about the chest and shoulders as she was rocked by the series of pulsing explosions that took place inside her.

Laughing, he flung both arms around her, nuzzling her nipples wildly, keeping her locked in his embrace while he came also, pulsing again and again deep within her. At last it was over and he lay back with his arms still about her, a sense of loss falling over him, as it sometimes did at such moments. Whenever it was this good, it left him feeling empty, as if he had visited a sweet land he knew he could never visit again.

Reaching up, he eased her off him, his hand lost in the rich abundance of her dark hair. She nudged his nose with hers and he nudged back, and soon they were laughing like children who have just run a long race together, but one they had both managed to win.

At last she sighed. "I have been waiting a long time for you, Skye Fargo."

"How's that?"

"I think it is as the women of the village have said: the spirit of my father has brought me the man who will rule with me. For a long time I thought that man was Dano. But it must be you, Fargo. As my father brought this valley to life with his science, you will do it with your will and your strong character." She cocked her head as she surveyed him. "You are big, as Father was. Your eyes have the same unwavering strength as did his. And you know how to hold a woman and make her want to be held by you, as my father held my mother."

Fargo saw at once that Carlotta was galloping far ahead of him. Not that the thought of bedding down permanently with a woman of her passion and loveliness was entirely unpleasant.

"Thanks for the thought, Carlotta," he told her carefully, "but I don't think you know me well enough to make that kind of an offer."

She laughed. "I know much about you. More than you think."

"You want to explain that?"

She propped her head up onto her palm and began to brush back his thick black hair. The feel of her cool fingers was pleasant on his skin. "I have a friend—a good friend—in Tularo. Emma Poole."

Fargo was astonished. "You know Emma?"

"Of course. I was in Tularo after you left and she told me you were after Federico."

"She tell you anything else?"

She poked him impishly. "What do you think?"

"Women can't keep a secret, I guess."

"Why should they? And anyway, Emma was right. You have passion, but you also have gentleness."

"You knew I was after Federico Silva," Fargo said, to get her off that tangent.

At once Carlotta grew serious. "Yes. But so were Dano and I."

"Maybe you better start at the beginning."

She propped a pillow between her and the bedstead. Then she scooted up and leaned back against it. Fargo rested his head in her lap and reached up to fondle her breasts, his big thumb flicking her nipples. Sighing contentedly, Carlotta began to tell him about Federico Silva, her voice soft, almost like a caress in the cool room.

Silva had been a scout and mountain man for many

years, she told Fargo, and it was during this time that he became a good friend of Carlotta's father, eventually taking a Papago wife and settling into the life of the valley. When Carlotta's father died and Silva lost his own wife, he drifted away from the valley, hiring himself out to settlers and others who needed a guide through the Superstitions. It was Carswell who had hired him to guide the mule train containing the silver through the mountains—at the same time making a deal with him to allow Carswell and his Apache allies to capture them.

But Silva contacted Carlotta to warn her of Carswell's plans. She and Dano told Silva to let Carswell think he was going along and that they would intercept the mule train before Carswell did.

"What did you want with the silver?" Fargo asked.

"It was not that we wanted it. We do not need it. But we did not want Carswell to have it. He was going to use it to bribe Jim Keller in Phoenix."

"Who's Jim Keller?"

"He is in charge of the Bureau of Indian Affairs in Arizona Territory."

"Go on."

"Carswell wanted the silver to bribe Keller so he would let Carswell take over the valley, bring in his cattle, and drive us out."

"And he figured this silver would be enough to bribe Keller?"

"Yes."

"What do you know about this Keller?"

"Nothing. But he is a white man, and so is Carswell. We could not take the chance."

"How did you know for sure this was Carswell's plan?"

She smiled. "That fool Carswell told Federico everything."

"Go on."

"But we were late. Carswell and his Apaches were still attacking the mule train when we arrived. Dano and his braves drove them off, but he could find no trace of Silva."

"I see. So when you heard from Emma that I was going after Silva, you thought there was a chance I might know where he was holing up?"

She nodded. "You told Emma you were going to see Carswell. Emma thought—as do many in Tularo—that you were a lawman or an agent sent by the silver company to find the stolen shipment."

"And that's why you followed me. You figured this way you just might find Federico or the treasure—or at least find out if Carswell had it."

Lifting his hand off her left breast, she placed it gently over her right one.

"Yes," she replied. "So Dano and I and five other braves took after you. By the time we found your trail, you were running from the Apaches. Dano and his braves discouraged them from trailing you, while I kept on your trail." Her voice softened. "I saw where you buried the woman Topaz."

Fargo said nothing as she went on: "But by nightfall I lost your trail when your tracks and those of the old prospector Clampett crossed."

Fargo nodded grimly. "Clampett was a good man. He took me to his cabin high in the cliffs. I don't see how anyone could have followed the trail he left, so don't feel bad."

She nodded. "It was not until the next day when Dano and I heard the sound of gunfire coming from the direction of Chimney Rock that we knew which way you had gone. By the time we got there, we saw Carswell and his three sons on foot. We chased them a ways, then picked up your trail."

"I know the rest," Fargo told her.

She shook her head and smiled. "Not all of it."

"I'm listening."

"You remember why we set after you? Well, we were right. It took us to Federico. After we found you, we went back and released his body from that cleft. Then Dano explored the rim above and discovered where Federico had left his wagon and the silver. His mules were dead in their traces and his horse had run off. The vultures had stripped clean the mules, but the silver was untouched."

"That means you've found the silver?"

"Yes."

"And are now very wealthy?"

"Not me, Skye. All of us who who live in this valley."

"Where is it now?"

"In our treasure room."

"Treasure room?"

"High on that cliff behind our village. Hidden inside the cliff is a great room, filled with treasure. Only a very few know the entrance."

"Filled with treasure? What kind?"

"For hundreds of years the Papago Indians have combed the Superstition Mountains for the bodies and abandoned wagons of lost settlers. In this way we have gathered much treasure. It is all in that room. Gold rings. Precious stones. Gold dust. Even the splendid swords and gold crosses belonging to the Spanish conquistadors who long ago tried to enslave the Papagos."

"You mean your people make a habit of combing the Superstition Mountains for gold watches and diamond brooches? From what I heard, those mountains were more or less owned by the Apaches, not the Papagos."

She suddenly glared down at him, eyes blazing. "Skye Fargo! The Papagos are not afraid of the Apache. It is the Apache who fear the Papagos. Many of our braves have enlisted with the U.S. Army as scouts to track the Apache. For centuries the Hohokam survived by never invoking the gods of war but always replying with great courage whenever war was forced upon them. Then their braves fought like beasts of prey." She paused thoughtfully. "Even so, when Papago warriors return from battle, I have heard they are forced to undergo a sixteen-day cure for insanity."

Fargo chuckled. He had suffered through his own share of battles, and it had left him a mite shook up as well. Could be it had left him a bit crazy too. "Guess maybe I can see the sense in that."

She gently lifted his head off her lap. "Yes, I suppose so."

As Fargo sat up, Carlotta swung off the bed and reached for her skirt and blouse. Pulling on his pants, Fargo thought he heard a horse whinny on the slope below the house. Frowning, he strapped on his gun belt and walked over to the window. Looking out, he saw Dano and another, smaller Indian. They were looking up at the window as they trudged up the slope through the cottonwoods.

And behind them followed the grim, mounted figures of Big John Carswell and his three boys.

6

Standing at the window beside Fargo, Carlotta gasped.

Carswell was holding a shotgun on the two Indians. Seth still had a dirty bandage around the wound on his upper arm Fargo had inflicted back in the canyon. The other two sons, Tom and Billy Joe, looked wolfish, eager, ready to pounce.

"They know we're in here," Carlotta said.

"That's what it looks like."

"What are we going to do?"

"Nothing much you can do. And if I start shooting, you'll be hurt, and so will Dano. Who's that Indian with him?"

"Pepito. He and two others are the only members of the tribe outside of myself and Dano who know where the treasure room is—and how to get to it. It is their duty to guard it night and day."

"It looks like Carswell knows you've got the silver, and maybe even where you've got it hid."

"That's not possible. Dano would never tell, nor would Pepito."

"Stay here. I'll go out and see what Carswell's up to."

"He might shoot you."

"He might try." Fargo patted his Colt. "But he won't get far if he does."

Clapping his hat on, Fargo left the bedroom, went downstairs, and stepped outside. As soon as Carswell and his boys saw him, they spread out and Carswell brought up his shotgun. The two Indians moved off to one side, anxious to get out of the line of fire. Fargo didn't blame them.

"Take it easy, Fargo," said Carswell. "We didn't come here for no gunplay."

"Then put down that shotgun."

"Now, that wouldn't be very smart, would it? Not after what you promised to do back there after we shot that prospector."

"What do you mean, we? It was you shot Clampett."

"You gonna listen to me or not?"

"I'll listen, Carswell, but I'm putting you on notice. I meant what I said back there in that canyon."

"Didn't think you was just beatin' your gums."

"Out with it. What're you after now?" Fargo asked.

"The silver."

"What's that got to do with me?"

"We followed that Papago girl and the rest of her redskins through the Superstitions. We found Silva's wagon." He smiled. "And the fresh tracks leadin' from it. The silver's here in this valley. I want it. If you don't come up with it, I'll do what I have to to get control of this valley."

"You mean you'll talk to the BIA agent in Phoenix."

"That's right."

"Pretty slick. Either way you slice it, you get the valley. If you *don't* get the silver, you'll blame the Papagos for stealing it and get the agent to sell them out. If you *do* get the silver, you'll likely bribe the son of a bitch to sell out the Papagos anyway."

Carswell looked long and hard at Fargo, then shrugged, the trace of an ironic smile on his face. "Since I know now you ain't no lawman, I figure it don't matter what you know or think you know. So I'll give it to you straight. Give me that silver and I just *might* let the Papagos keep their land. That's the chance they'll have to take. If you don't give me the silver, they got no chance at all. Hell, the evidence is clear. Papagos attacked that mule train."

"Just because you say so?"

"No, because it's Papago arrows stickin' from them corpses."

"You could have used Papago arrows—you or your Apaches."

Carswell shrugged. "Sure I could've. But it ain't the truth works in this world, Fargo. It's what the right people think is the truth."

"And you've got the right people on your side, that it?"

"No more palaver, Fargo. Where's the silver?"

"It ain't here, not in this valley."

Carswell's eyes narrowed. "You mean maybe it's stashed somewhere *above* the valley, hey? Maybe in a secret place?"

"Meaning you'd best ride on out of here, Carswell, and keep on riding. While you still can, that is."

Carswell frowned at Fargo's words.

Then Fargo stepped back and pointed down the slope through the cottonwoods. Carswell swung around in his saddle. A party of six or seven mounted Papago Indians, their faces bright with war paint, were moving in a wide band up the slope toward the cottonwoods. Though armed only with bows and arrows, they would be more than a match for the four Carswells, especially with Fargo's sidearm to lend a hand.

Carswell flung back around and lashed his horse, bolting on past Fargo, his three sons roweling furiously after him. As they disappeared over the hill, Carswell called back, "You ain't seen the last of us, Fargo!"

Carlotta hurried from the house to join Fargo as Dano and Pepito went to meet the warriors charging up through the cottonwoods, and with an upraised arm halted them. Disappointed, the mounted braves pulled up, then milled about for a moment before loping back down through the cottonwoods.

Dano's eyes were gleaming in triumph as he turned to Fargo. "You see how it is, Fargo? This man Carswell see braves working in the fields like squaws, so he think we do not know how to put on war paint. He ride into our village like conquistador of old time, with no fear—only contempt for our people. Now he see the truth."

Dano turned to Carlotta then. "I see Carswell come and give alarm. Then I go find Pepito. That is when Carswell find us. He make us take him to you. Many in the fields see you take Fargo to the house of your father."

"You did well, Dano, but you heard Carswell. He will come back."

"This time with Apaches," said Pepito.

Carlotta turned to Fargo. "Skye, I heard what he said from the house. And he will do it. He will go to that agent in Phoenix."

"Just keep your people ready," Fargo told her. "I won't be long."

"Where are you going?"

"A town I rode through on my way to Tularo. Phoenix."

The Bureau of Indian Affairs was on the second floor of the Express Office. There were two rooms. The first had a desk, file cabinets, and a thin, bespectacled clerk. He was busy shuffling papers on his desk, which meant he had heard Fargo's footsteps on the stairs.

"Your boss in, sonny?" Fargo asked the clerk.

"Yes."

"Fine. I'd like to see him."

"Do you have an appointment, sir?"

"No, I don't have an appointment. But if he's in there, I want to see him. I rode a long ways and I don't want to stand around jawing with you all day. I got better things to do, sonny."

A tall figure abruptly filled the doorway of the inner office, and Fargo found himself looking at a man in his middle thirties with a coal-black beard and mustache, clipped close, and a full head of hair. The man was wearing black pants, white shirt, and vest. The shirt collar was unbuttoned and the fellow was chewing on the stump of a cigar.

"Let him in, Alfred," the agent said. "It has been a dull afternoon. I am sure this gentleman will liven things up a bit."

The clerk swallowed and nodded.

As Fargo moved past the clerk's desk, he extended his hand to the agent. "Mr. Keller?"

"Yes," the agent replied, taking Fargo's hand and shaking it energetically.

"My name is Fargo, Skye Fargo."

"It's a pleasure, Mr. Fargo. Won't you come in to my office?"

Fargo followed Keller into his office and sat down in a wooden chair beside the man's desk. Keller circled behind it, pushed a box of cigars toward Fargo, then leaned back comfortably in his swivel chair.

Fargo selected a cigar, sliced off one end with his bowie, and lit up. When Keller saw that Fargo was comfortable, he smiled quizzically.

"I couldn't help overhearing, Mr. Fargo. You told my clerk you rode a long ways. I am anxious to find out why."

"You know a John Carswell?"

The agent frowned. "Big John?"

"He's made some threats to the Papago Indians. I was hoping you might be able to give them—through me—some assurances they have nothing to worry about."

Keller quickly leaned over in his chair so he could see the clerk. Then, straightening, he winked at Fargo. "I suggest we repair to the saloon across the street. It is much cooler there and a man can refresh himself while conducting the government's business. A delightful arrangement."

Fargo got to his feet and followed the agent from his office and down the stairs. The saloon was cool and reasonably quiet. They found a table in a corner. Fargo ordered beer. The two men hoisted their steins in a salute, then drank deeply. Wiping the suds off his black beard, Keller said, "Back there in my office you said Carswell made some threats?"

"That's right."

"Maybe you better explain."

"Carswell wants to take over the entire Papago valley southwest of the Superstitions."

"And just how does he plan to accomplish that?"

"He seems to think you'd listen to him—for a consideration, that is—and become his ally."

"I see." Keller lifted the stein and drank. "You mean he plans to bribe me."

"That or make accusations—unfounded, of course, but certain to get people stirred up—against the Papagos, create a climate, you might say, that would allow you to give him what he wants."

"The entire valley, you say." Keller shook his head in exasperation. "The man's arrogance is astonishing. Equaled, perhaps, only by his stupidity. Fargo, I know Carswell. Only too well. He and that unholy clan of his are little more than a ravening wolf pack. I have not dealt with the man recently, but whenever I have had occasion to do so, I made it a practice to count my fingers afterward to make sure I still had them."

"Then you have no intention of throwing in with him?"

"I'd rather throw in with a rattlesnake." Keller shook his head in disgust. "Let me explain something, Fargo. We've got ourselves a civil war heating up back

East, and the War Department's been recalling our troops, closing our forts, pulling out. Now, from what I hear, the Comanches and the Kiowa—not to mention the Apaches—are rubbing their hands in glee as they watch us pull out. They think they've licked us, and now for them it's going to be like old times. Raiding for horseflesh, women, and goods, and for the pure hellish pleasure ot it."

"Hell, Keller, these here Papagos sure don't match that description."

Keller leaned forward. "Precisely what I am getting at. If there's one thing Washington doesn't need right now, it's another tribe of aborigines kicking up its heels. So far, the Papagos have been our allies whenever it came to dealing with the Apaches. If we need scouts to track an Apache war party, we call on the Papagos. When it comes to Apaches, they can track one across water. Meanwhile, the Papagos stay in that valley and other valleys north of there. They farm the land and keep their noses clean. They make baskets and grow wheat, for Christ's sake! And we don't hear a peep out of them."

Fargo chuckled. "I gather you're happy with them."

"Just the way they are. And not just me. The bureau feels the same way. So do all the Quaker women bemoaning the terrible plight of the western aborigines. Hell, to hear them talk, the Papagos are the only real success we've had out here."

Fargo leaned back in his seat. "Let me see if I understand you, Keller. The last thing you—or Washington—wants is to stir up a peaceful tribe like the Papagos. So if we have to go a little rough on Big John

Carswell to keep the peace, it won't be any skin off your nose."

"If I could, I'd give you a medal. Just don't bother me with the details."

Fargo slapped a coin down onto his table. "Another beer?"

"That would be most generous, Mr. Fargo."

"Good. I have a long hot dusty trail ahead of me."

The beer came, and five minutes later Fargo was back on his pinto riding out of town. After waving to him once, Keller strode casually on across to the street, wishing that all his problems with the Indians could be solved this pleasantly.

It was dusk and Carlotta was sitting in a wicker chair in front of her adobe hut as she watched Fargo return on horseback. Her thoughts were in a delightful —yet troubling—confusion. Though she was almost certain that the spirit of her father had sent Skye Fargo to be her husband, she found herself, unaccountably, thinking of Dano.

Not long before, in the hills above the valley, Carlotta had called the braves together for a war council. But she had not known what to say. Then Dano stepped forward and addressed the braves. At once his strong voice and his eloquent words had filled all their bellies with fire. And watching him, Carlotta knew that Dano must be the one to lead them in battle against the hated Carswell and his Apache allies.

For the first time Dano had appeared to Carlotta as much more than her childhood friend, and "brother" Carlotta's father and mother had found crying in a basket outside their door one morning. No longer was

Dano the patient, devoted little pest who followed her dutifully around the village like a faithful dog.

Now Dano was a man. And she was a woman.

The sound of the lone horse's hooves now reached her ears. It was almost completely dark now as she got to her feet and watched Dano and Pepito come from their hut by the cliff to greet Fargo. As they passed Carlotta on their way, she joined them, finding herself walking close beside Dano.

Dano glanced at her. And the moment his large, fiery eyes caught hers, she felt her knees go weak.

Yes. She was a woman. Dano's woman.

But what of Skye Fargo? she asked herself in despair. Already she had told him that he was to be her husband. How could she possibly satisfy both men?

Dismounting in front of them, Fargo wasted no time telling what he had learned in Phoenix.

". . . and what this means," said Fargo, finishing up, "is you can defend yourself without any interference from the Bureau of Indian Affairs. Carswell cannot count on help from Keller. It also means you can't count on any help from Keller, either. He's staying completely out of it."

"Already Dano has spoken to our braves," Carlotta said. "They are ready."

"Good. I figure Carswell won't waste much time."

"He is crazy," Carlotta said. "He and his three sons cannot defeat the Papagos that live in this valley."

"He and his sons won't try it alone. They'll be bribing the Apaches to join them, more than likely. When he makes his move, he is not going to do it without a considerable force at his back." Fargo paused and looked hard at both Indians. "Now, what I'd like to know is how come Carswell knows about that hiding place—or room—up on the cliff. You heard him, Dano. He seemed to know all about it."

"The Apaches have told him," Dano said. "It is the only way he could know. They have long known of our treasure. Once they attack and try to climb to the caverns to take it from us. They lose many braves that time. Now they say the bluecoats are defeated. They say the white-eyes leave the land to the Apaches, like the Spaniards before them. So now it is good time for them to buy from Comancheros new long rifles that shoot many bullets without reloading. The Apaches then will ride forth and punish their enemies."

"Spencer repeaters, they mean," said Fargo.

"If they get such weapons," said Pepito, "they will kill many."

"Including Papagos," said Fargo.

"But for that," said Carlotta, "they will need money."

"Or silver," Fargo added, "and whatever else you've got hidden away in that treasure room."

"It does not matter," said Pepito. "We will defend the silver with our lives. They will not have it."

"And with the silver *we* will buy such weapons," Carlotta told Fargo. "It will not matter then that we do not have as many war ponies as the Apache."

"You're sure this treasure room of yours is well-hidden?"

Dano smiled. "Yes."

"Take me to it," said Fargo. "I'd like to see for myself."

Carlotta looked at Pepito, who in turn glanced at Dano. Dano considered a moment, then shrugged. "Let

123

Fargo see where we keep our treasure. Then he will see we speak the truth."

Pepito was the last up the rope ladder. He turned and pulled it up after them, its wooden slats striking the sides of the cliff face. Meanwhile, Dano lit a torch and led Fargo into the cavern, Carlotta on his heels. Behind them, Pepito followed, holding a second torch.

At once a Papago warrior confronted them, a lance in his hands; behind them a second warrior materialized, his arrow already fitted to his bowstring.

Pepito spoke to them sharply.

The two guardians melted away into the shadowed recesses of the cavern. Dano led them into a tunnel so low they were forced to stoop almost double until they came to a larger passageway, which led eventually to a fork. They went left, continued for a considerable distance, and pulled up at last in a room that contained what appeared to be a primitive altar. On both sides of it lit torches were stuck in the wall, the smoke from them coiling out through tiny windows high above the altar.

Standing in the center of the room, Fargo looked around. In addition to the altar, there was a table, some chairs, and stores of corn flung in one corner. And that was all.

"Some treasure trove," Fargo commented ironically as he glanced at the corn.

Carlotta smiled and glanced at Pepito. The Indian went over to the right wall, touched a portion of it, then another portion, his hands tracing a light, complicated pattern impossible to follow. Abruptly the wall swung away, revealing a narrow doorway. Fargo swore softly in admiration as he followed after Dano through the doorway and into another large room.

Once he was inside the other room, Pepito performed as before—and the huge wall swung back into place. Fargo looked at the wall closely. It was impossible to see where it had broken and swung away. Indeed, no wall had ever appeared more solid to him than this one, yet it had swung open as lightly as a feather and swung back into place just as smoothly.

"Tell me something," Fargo said to Pepito. "Is it as difficult to get back out through this wall as it was to get in?"

Pepito frowned, not quite sure what Fargo meant.

Carlotta answered for Pepito. "Yes, it is," she told Fargo. "Even I cannot do what Pepito can. Only he knows which sections on the wall to press and the correct combination of pressures it takes to open this wall—on either side."

Fargo was impressed. Carlotta had explained earlier that her father was the one who had discovered these secret passageways, and from the research he did, he was able to ascertain that they were the work of those ancient empire builders, the Hohokam. These Hohokam must have been some people, and whichever Hohokam it was who built this particular network of tunnels and rooms, he had a diabolical cunning equal to those who built the pyramids.

Again it was Dano who led the way. This time they were following him along a descending, circular tunnel that disgorged them onto another large chamber, on the far end of which loomed a huge door bolted shut and secured with the largest lock Fargo had ever seen. When they reached it, Pepito produced a key, unlocked the bolt, and shot it to the right. It took both Pepito and Dano to tug the door open.

Stepping into the room beyond, Dano halted just inside and held his torch high to show the way for Carlotta and Fargo. Carlotta took Fargo's hand and led him into the cavernous room the Hohokam had hollowed out of solid rock. It was the size of a large living room in a good-sized ranchhouse.

The only difference here was the astounding, dazzling carpet sitting on this particular floor. It was made up of gold and silver goblets, candlesticks, elaborate jewelry, and tiny casks, along with trinkets of every size and description, all piled to a height of several feet and in some places even higher. Fargo stood for a moment, transfixed. As Pepito and Dano stepped up beside him, their moving torches caused myriad shafts of gold and silver—and in some cases the icy fire of diamonds—to wink back at him. In fact, so dazzling was the play of reflected light from the two torches that at times Fargo found himself squinting.

"Where's the silver?" he asked Dano.

Dano pointed to a corner.

Fargo looked over there and saw four grain sacks. Out of the topmost one spilled a gleaming hoard of silver coins. He walked over to inspect the coins; then, with a wink at Carlotta, he took up a couple and pocketed them.

"To help me pay for that trip to Phoenix," he said.

Then Fargo let his gaze return to the treasure. He saw gold crosses, elaborate candle holders, dinner plates, elaborate serving dishes encrusted with precious stones, jewelry of every size and description, headbands of gold, ornate, pendulous earrings, bracelets, trunks overflowing with gleaming trinkets. Fargo lost count.

A king's ranson? Hell, this room contained a hell of a lot more than that! Fargo recalled the tales of conquistadors who had combed the Southwest for such wealth. Could this valley possibly have been the site of one of those fabled Seven Cities for which Coronado had searched so long?

Fargo shook his head in wonder. Of course Carswell wanted this valley. But it wasn't only the Papagos' lush valley grasses he wanted. He was certain of it now. The Apaches *had* told Carswell of this fabulous hoard. The silver shipment was just an excuse, a pittance he was throwing into the pot, so he could make his play and rake in this treasure as well. And to get his hands on it, Carswell would stop at nothing.

Squinting suddenly, Fargo noticed what appeared to be another entrance to the room. It was in a far corner and resembled the entrance to a cave. A man would have to stoop pretty low to get through it.

"Where's that lead?" he asked Carlotta, pointing to it.

"It is another entrance," she said. "It leads to the top of the cliff."

"Why do you need it?"

"My father thought of it," said Carlotta. "In case of attack, we can remove the treasure before our attackers reach this room." She smiled. "Then all they would find is an empty chamber."

Fargo frowned. "How many know of it?"

"We who are here—and two more, Orzoko and Tamio, the two guards you saw before we entered the tunnel. Like Pepito, they guard this chamber, day and night."

Fargo glanced at Pepito. He, along with Dano, was the keeper of the treasure, you might say, which meant he had quite a responsibility—as did those other two Papagos outside. The question was, Could they be trusted? The way it stood now, the entire Papago nation had to assume, as Carlotta and Dano obviously did, that they could.

Fargo glanced back over at this second entrance. "Could we leave here that way?" he asked.

"Yes," said Carlotta, "but it is a steep climb through a very narrow passageway."

Fargo nodded and looked back once again at the extravagant wealth spread out before him. "One thing I'm not clear on," he told Carlotta. "If you have all this wealth, why in blazes don't you use it to buy everything you need? Spencer rifles. Food. Horses."

Carlotta smiled. "My father tried that. When first he started repairing the canals, he traded two gold goblets and a very valuable necklace in Phoenix for supplies and materials. Two Spanish prospectors heard of the goblets and the necklace. They followed him to the valley."

"What happened to them?"

Dano spoke up. "They not leave this place alive, Fargo."

Carlotta explained. "They tried to force one of the Indians to show them where the treasure was hidden. When we tried to stop them, they shot one of our people. My father had to kill them."

Fargo could understand that. "Your father must have realized then what he had almost done. Any more such trades, and others would come, searching for the source of those trinkets. And the next time maybe you wouldn't have been so lucky."

Carlotta nodded somberly. "From that time on, it was forbidden to trade for goods using any of the wealth contained in this room. But the silver," she went on, "that is a different story. This the Comancheros will take in payment for weapons. They would know where we got it and would say nothing. The devil himself would have no trouble trading with them, as long as he had enough silver or gold to satisfy them."

Fargo nodded, then looked back once more at the incredible, gleaming carpet of wealth.

In that moment he understood perfectly the dilemma of Carlotta's people. Though they had here a treasure beyond the wildest imaginings of poets and storytellers, they could not use it, for once they began dipping into this hoard, it would inevitably bring them death and pillage and eventual expulsion from this fair valley as hordes of prospectors and hard cases of every nationality and persuasion swarmed in for their share. Carswell was only a foretaste of what they could expect if it became generally known what lay hidden in this chamber.

Now Fargo understood perfectly Carswell's intent. The difficulty was that Carswell would not be nearly as easy to deal with as those two luckless prospectors.

7

Fargo saw the dust cloud ten miles from Tularo.

He had been riding all day, hard. Reaching Tularo in two days by skirting the Superstition Mountains meant he had been forced to keep a steady, unrelenting pace. It had also meant riding through Apache lands. A moment before, pausing on a ridge to search the trail behind him, he saw what first appeared to be only a small cloud sitting on the horizon.

But he sat his pinto in the blazing heat and let his keen eyes study the cloud carefully until he saw for sure that it was a low-hanging cloud of dust. He took off his hat and mopped his brow, then set the hat down more firmly onto his head and leaned over to pat the pinto's sweaty neck. The Apaches had finally spotted him and were strung out, pushing their mounts hard to overtake him.

Fargo spoke quietly to the pinto. "We're almost there now, and there's water and grain and a cool stall waiting. Don't give up on me now."

The pinto tossed his head, then shook it for emphasis, his bits jingling. Laughing, Fargo gave the pinto his rein and the pony fled down the short slope to the wash below. In a moment he was covering the ground in his typical ground-devouring stride, while Fargo—in order to ease the pony's task—leaned well forward in his saddle to keep his weight over the pony's withers.

An hour later Fargo saw ahead of him the dirty wash of a river and knew then that he was within striking distance of Tularo. He gave the pinto his head and plunged down the slope toward it, his knee nudging the animal in the direction of a sandbar extending far out into the stream. Racing onto it, he let the pony plunge into the water. With solid even strokes, the powerful animal paddled across the shallow stream, then broke out onto the far bank, pausing only to shake its mane. In a moment he was again racing over the scrub land, his damp mane and tail almost straight out.

Not long after, the pinto was digging up the side of a steep gully when Fargo caught movement and a gleam of brown hide in the brush to his right. He ducked and pulled his horse around. At almost the same moment he heard the twang of a bowstring. Something small and black flashed across his vision. Flinging himself from his saddle, he pulled the pony back down into the gully.

Then he snaked his Sharps from its scabbard, loaded swiftly, and scrambled back up the slope. When he reached the top of the gully, he saw a drift log sitting on the embankment farther down. He used his knees and elbows to pull himself behind it and in a moment was peering beyond its butt end with his rifle loaded and ready. Catching the fleeting image of a painted face behind a patch of scrub, he tightened his finger on the trigger. The Sharps kicked in his hands and he heard the deep *thunk* as the bullet found solid flesh. A second later the Apache rolled out of the brush and came to rest with his eyes wide to the sun, his arms outstretched.

One down, how many more to go?

He knew this was not the main war party of the Apaches trailing him—only an advance body of two or three braves who had probably sacrificed their mounts in order to overtake and slow him down, if they could not kill him.

Leaving the protection of the log, the Trailsman inched about ten yards farther out onto the flat until he was almost completely hidden by a thick growth of bunch grass. As he settled in, a small cloud of locusts rose from the top of the grass. To a watching Apache, a dead giveaway.

But there was nothing Fargo could do about that now. He kept his head down and waited, every now and then wiping his sweaty palms on his shirt front and blinking to keep the sweat out of his eyes. He became aware of the oppressively hot sand beneath him and the burning sun on his back. Sweat was gathering in his armpits and trickling down his sides.

About twenty-five yards ahead of him over a clump of brush, a crow wheeled and seemed about to light. Instead, it veered away sharply. Fargo smiled coldly and unholstered his Colt. Aiming low, he fired into the brush, spacing his shots deliberately.

A faint cry came from it. He aimed in the direction of the cry and fired again.

He waited. He had wounded someone. But how badly? And how many Apaches were in there? He reloaded quickly, then lay still, ears alert.

A scorpion poked into sight from the sand a couple of feet from his head and began to scuttle toward him. It was a big one. More than likely another buthid. With one swift blow from the butt of his Colt, Fargo smashed it. Then he heard the faint scuttle of movement to his left. Swinging his head, he saw two more scorpions. Despite the heat, a chill fell over him.

He had crawled into a nest of the bastards!

Keeping his composure with some difficulty, he heaved a stone at the brush he had fired upon. There was no response. He flung another one and heard it rattle through the brush. While every nerve in his body screamed out for him to jump up and haul ass, he kept himself quiet for another minute or so, then slowly lifted his body and, keeping low, ran in a quick zigzag toward the brush, then circled around behind it.

The Apache lay still, his head, neck, and shoulder glistening with blood. Ants and swarming flies had found the body already. Two of Fargo's bullets had caught the Apache, one high in the chest, the other on the right side of the Apache's head just below the ear. The exit wounds in each case were large and ugly.

Fargo took off his hat and mopped his brow. Hurrying back to the gully, he mounted the pinto and urged him up the slope. On the tip of the gulley he looked back.

Judging from the dust, the Apaches were less than three miles behind him now. But once he was beyond the next ridge, he would be in sight of Tularo. Despite the efforts of those two dead Apaches, he was going to make it.

It was near sundown when his lathered Ovaro carried Fargo into Tularo. Both horse and rider were gray with dust. Dismounting, Fargo led the pinto into the livery and told the hostler to water the horse carefully, go easy on the oats, and give him a very good and thorough rubdown. Then he tossed him a silver coin that caused the hostler's eyes to pop.

Trudging wearily across the street to the hotel, Fargo found the old cowpoke still behind the desk. As he finished signing the register, he looked up and saw Emma Poole standing in an open doorway behind the desk clerk.

She tipped her head and smiled as she looked him up and down. "I'll bet you could use another bath, Mr. Fargo," she said.

"I was afraid you'd never ask."

An hour and a half later, they lay in each other's arms letting the desert wind blow in through the open window, cooling their flushed, naked bodies.

"That was enough for now," Emma told Fargo, brushing his damp hair back off his forehead. "We've got all night."

Fargo didn't reply. No sense in breaking her heart.

"Big John's in town."

"Oh?"

"He came back from Phoenix fit to be tied. He rounded up some notorious hard cases, then he and his sons got good and drunk and beat up a bartender in the Big Spur Saloon. The four of them're sleeping it off now in the Miner's Rest down the street."

That was interesting. Very interesting. Fargo had little difficulty imagining Carswell's surprise and then his dismay at the scorn Keller must have heaped on him when he threw Big John out of his office. All during his ride back from Phoenix, Carswell must have been fuming, aware that now he would have to play it straight—no more tricks. If he wanted that valley and the treasure it contained, he would have to launch an unprovoked attack on a band of peaceful, friendly Indians, with the hated Apaches as his sole allies.

But employing Apaches in this part of Arizona wouldn't be wise. Not openly. And that would explain why Carswell had just finished recruiting the hard cases. Carswell would take the treasure—if not the valley—with hired guns. He had no choice. If he wanted that Midas hoard, it was the only card he had left to play.

"You say Big John's staying at the Miner's Rest?"

She nodded. "Someone must have told them we boiled the sheets clean here every day. Them Carswells wouldn't know how to sleep without seam squirrels to keep 'em company."

Fargo chuckled.

"Skye, what happened to Topaz? The word around town is she ran off with you."

Fargo told her everything—from the moment he first came on to the girl, to her death as the result of Teenaro's knife wound. When he had finished, Emma said nothing as she leaned her head back, sobered.

After a while, she asked, "You movin' on now you know that feller Silva ain't the one you was after?"

"I still have a score to settle."

"With Carswell?"

"Yes."

"Because of Topaz?"

Fargo had to be careful. He did not want Emma to know about the existence of the Hohokam treasure. "Not only Topaz and Ken Santana," he replied, "but the death of a wily old prospector who took me in when the Apaches were on my tail. An old man named Clampett."

"Why, I heard of him! But I thought he had died long ago."

"He's dead now."

"Carswell killed him?"

"Yes. He probably thought he was shooting at me."

"But how can you stop Big John? Do you have any kind of plan?"

"It ain't much of a plan—just find the son of a bitch and do what I can to slow him down."

She stirred, pushed away from him, then sat up. "My god, Skye. You mean you're goin' gunnin' for the whole crew? Right here in Tularo?"

"That I hadn't planned on. I had no way of knowin' Carswell would be here when I rode in. I expected I'd find him at his ranch. I was just passin' through here on my way there. But he's here, so I figure maybe now is as good a time as any to start nipping at his heels."

"Skye, there's *four* of them!"

"Don't fret, woman. I've taken on tougher bravos than that fellow and lived to tell about it."

"I bet you rassle grizzlies just to work up an appetite."

He grinned at her. "Grizzlies and crazy dames."

She reached out and grabbed him roughly, pulling him close. "Well, dammit! Before you go anywhere, rassle with this here crazy dame first. I want as much of you as I can get while the gettin's good."

Laughing, Fargo rolled over onto Emma and dropped his lips to hers. They yawned open hungrily, and he found he wasn't nearly as tired as he had thought he was. . . .

"What was that?" Emma cried.

But Fargo was already off the bed, his six-gun in his hand, peering out the open window down at the street below. It was a little past midnight. The moon was high and he could clearly see the main street and buildings lining it.

He could see also the Apaches, galloping full tilt into town while others on foot padded silently along the boardwalk. A window shattered. A second gunshot sounded, and then came the war cry of the Apaches as the main body swept into Tularo. Fargo saw a white man leap for a doorway and begin pouring lead at the hard-charging Apaches.

An Apache spun to the ground as another Indian charged the man. Before the Apache reached him, a rifle shot from somewhere below Fargo lifted the brave off his horse. By now the street below the hotel window was alive with a milling crowd of whooping Apaches, busy shooting out windows and gathering up the few horses still standing at the hitch racks.

A group of five or more Apaches dismounted suddenly and, firing wildly, charged into the saloon across the street. Fargo heard the sound of shattering glass, the muffled thunder of gunshots, and the crash of broken furniture. A moment later, the triumphant Apaches streamed back out of the saloon carrying bottles of booze in their fists. They flung themselves on their ponies and began to lift their bottles high. Then they began to race up and down the street shooting at anything that moved, or anything that stood out boldly enough to make a target.

Fargo ducked back out of the window and pulled on his pants. Strapping his gun belt around his waist, he told Emma to stay put and slipped from the room. The ancient desk clerk was keeping his head down behind the front desk, an ancient pistol in his hand. Fargo wondered if he was getting ready to shoot himself or an Apache. Striding past him, Fargo stepped out onto the porch in time to see an Apache attempting to gallop up the porch steps.

Fargo's Colt thundered and caught the Apache twice in the chest. The Apache, still on his pony, turned the animal and, leaning awkwardly in his saddle, galloped off down the street. A bare, gleaming torso caught Fargo's eye on his right. He swung about just as the Apache lifted his bow. Throwing himself flat, Fargo blasted the Apache off the porch. From behind came the quick slap of moccasins. Rolling over, Fargo fired up at the Apache, catching him in the gut. Like dark wine from a punctured wineskin, blood gouted from his bowels.

Still clutching at his darkening breechclout, the Apache staggered on past Fargo, then toppled face-down off the porch. Fargo sat up and looked around for more Apaches. But the immediate storm was apparently over. He slipped off the porch and hurried down the sidewalk. Ahead of him, whirling about in the dust of the street, the drunken Apaches were still visible, while from the shadows and alleys up and down the street came the townsmen's deadly fire. If the Apaches didn't light out with their whiskey and stolen horses pretty soon, it would become a turkey shoot.

Abruptly, one of the Apaches pulled his horse up and raised his rifle. The rest of the Apaches halted also. The sporadic gunfire ceased abruptly as everyone waited to see what the Apache chief wanted.

"Carswell," the Apache cried. "It is Chief Kintaro! Your blood brother!"

A voice on the other side of the street farther down bellowed, "You're crazy, Chief. Get the hell out of here."

"It is you we want, Big John. We burn town if you not come with us."

"Ride out of here. I got nothin' to do with you."

"You say you brother to the Apache. You say you make Apache rich soon. But now you take silver."

"I ain't got it, I tell you!"

"You give it to Papagos. So now you come with us. You help Apache take it back."

A shot rang out from the shadows where Carswell was crouching. The Apache chieftain slumped momentarily, then lowered his lance and with a chilling war cry spurred toward Carswell. From all sides, a murderous fusillade opened up on the chief, and he and his horse went down before he reached Carswell. Seeing this, the rest of the Apaches, some riding double, wheeled their mounts and rode out, driving their stolen horses before them.

They were gone swiftly.

Fargo, trotting steadily down the street, pulled up alongside the downed Apache. Before breathing his last, Chief Kintaro had buried his lance into the building close by the spot where Carswell had crouched. The chief lay now, faceup, his dark chest marbled with blood.

Carswell stepped out of the shadows, his three sons alongside him. They all looked healthy enough, and as mean as disturbed rattlers.

"Well, well," Carswell said, "look what the dog drug over."

Fargo smiled. "Back from Phoenix, I see."

Carswell's face went cold, his eyes glowing with sudden fury, Fargo's remark helping him put it all together. Fargo was the one who had gone to warn Keller.

"Damn you for a meddlin' fool, Fargo! I should'a killed you the moment you rode into my place. Instead, I fed you and gave you a place to sleep!"

Fargo laughed. "That's right, and the woman you thought was your wife."

That crack hushed the crowd. Carswell took a step forward. "I'll kill you for that."

"What's stopping you right now, Big John?"

Glancing quickly at his sons, Carswell began to back up. His sons spread out. At once everyone standing around forgot the Apaches, some of whom were still lying wounded in the darkness, and moved hastily out of the line of fire. At that moment the sheriff huffed up and started to say something.

"Stay out of this, Hammond," Carswell barked. "This son of a bitch is in with them Papagos. He knows where that shipment of silver is."

The sheriff and his deputy backed hastily away.

Fargo spoke up then, loud enough for everyone to hear. "From what this dead Apache spit out before you killed him, Carswell, you're in with the Apaches."

"There ain't a man here'd believe such a thing. That was a lie!"

"Apaches don't lie, Carswell. They make war, they kill, they torture their prisoners, and they steal horses. But they don't lie."

Fargo heard rising murmurs of agreement from the darkness behind him.

"What about that, Carswell?" someone shouted.

Other remarks followed and an angry chorus erupted. As if to still the uproar, Carswell went down on one knee and drew his big Colt. Fargo threw himself behind the dead Apache just as Carswell fired. The bullet slammed into the ground in front of the Apache and ricocheted up into his lifeless torso.

A hail of bullets from Carswell's sons whined off into the darkness as Fargo returned first Carswell's, then Seth's fire. He saw Seth drop his weapon and grab his hand. Fargo swung his gun over and fired at Tom, who was still standing upright in clear sight. The round caught Tom in the head, shattering his skull. Holding it with both hands, Tom staggered back a few steps, then sank to the ground.

A bullet caught Fargo in his left thigh, slamming him to one side. He felt no pain, only a numb heaviness where it had hit. Dazedly, he lifted his Colt to continue the firefight, but the Carswells had broken and were racing down the street.

All except Tom Carswell.

A moment later, Carswell's clan and four or five other riders galloped out of a back alley and headed out of Tularo. Slowly, painfully, Fargo pushed himself upright and examined his left thigh. It was just a flesh wound, but it was bleeding something fierce. Out of the darkness rushed Emma. Ripping her silk petticoat into strips, she wound it around the wound, stanching the flow. Then she helped him turn about and move back down the street toward the hotel.

As they moved through the night, the townsmen came out of hiding to inspect the Apache corpses and drag them off the street. A few gunshots sounded as wounded Apaches were sent on to Apache heaven. The window in Stella's Eats had been shattered and one saloon was a shambles. The town looked as if a twister had struck, and Fargo knew Tularo would look a hell of a lot worse in the bright light of morning.

"Tom Carswell's dead," Emma said.

"I know."

"You must feel awful. Tom was just a big oaf. It was Big John you wanted."

"Emma, do you want to know what Tom was doing the first time I laid eyes on him?"

She winced. "Go ahead. Tell me."

"He was lowering his britches, getting ready to climb onto Topaz. And Topaz was on the ground in front of him, unconscious."

Emma made a face and said nothing more until they reached the hotel. "Well, then," she remarked finally as she helped him up the porch steps and into the hotel, "at least you've slowed Carswell down. He'll be a-grievin' for his son now."

The numbing shock of his gunshot wound was beginning to wear off by this time, and Fargo was in too much discomfort to reply. But he knew that the honest truth of it was he had not really slowed Carswell at all. Carswell would spend little or no time grieving for his son, whose body he had not hesitated to leave behind.

Carswell was a man who never looked back and cared not a damn for any other living creature—neither wife, brother, nor son. All Fargo had succeeded in doing was to rile him and maybe send him after the Papagos and their treasure just that much sooner.

8

Fargo was sitting on the hotel porch watching the cleanup, his chair tipped back against the wall, his good leg propped on the porch railing. The wound under the thick bandage wrapped about his left thigh throbbed dully, but Fargo barely noticed it.

As he looked about, he realized he had underestimated the damage the Apaches had done and how bad the town would look, come morning. At the moment the air was filled with the sound of hammers, the buzz of handsaws, and the voices of men at work calling to one another. There was an almost constant tinkle of glass as broken windowpanes were being smashed to clear the sashes. The number of windowpanes that had to be replaced was obviously a bonanza for the owner of the general store. Throughout the morning Fargo watched a steady stream of men carrying empty sashes into the store.

No one from Carswell's ranch had yet come for Tom Carswell's body, but the undertaker had carted it off first thing, willing to gamble that Big John would eventually reimburse him. Even so, there were men in town already making book that Carswell would not even bother to reclaim his son's body for a decent burial. Meanwhile, the eight dead Apaches had been flung onto the pile of horse manure in the alley beside the livery stable.

One good thing had come out of all this: what had been a suspicion before was now a virtual certainty. The Apaches had indeed been working with Carswell. Everyone in Tularo knew it, and soon that knowledge would spread throughout Arizona, making Big John Carswell an outcast.

But even more important, it was now clear that the Apaches would not be joining Carswell in any future attacks on the Papagos. The alliance was finished. And for his part, Carswell had better grow eyes in the back of his head. If the Apaches ever got hold of him now, his death would not be a quick one.

Shading her eyes, Emma Poole stepped onto the porch. "Look," she said, pointing.

Fargo glanced in the direction she indicated and immediately righted his chair. A white flag fluttering from his lance, a venerable, mounted Apache was leading eight other mounted Apaches into town.

"They've come for the dead," Fargo said, getting carefully to his feet, then limping over to a post to lean on.

Emma came to a halt beside him, her eyes somber. The sound of activity up and down the street gradually ceased as the workmen caught sight of the approaching delegation. A waiting silence fell over Tularo. A few women with children scurried into the stores, dragging their children in after them, while the men snatched up weapons and waited. Most of the townspeople, however, stood where they were and watched silently as the Apache continued on down the main street.

A fellow wearing a carpenter's apron hurried out into the middle of the street, close by the livery, and waited for the Apaches to reach him.

"Who's that?" Fargo asked.

"Jason Whittington. Last night he was elected president of the town council, after the sheriff and his deputy rode out with Carswell."

"Well, well."

Whittington was a man of solid dimensions, with a drooping black mustache and piercing eyes. When the Indians got close enough, he held up his hand to halt them. The old Apache hauled back on his reins. The other Apaches kept going until they flanked him, then they too halted.

As Whittington began to speak to the old Apache, a tall fellow in a white stetson who had arrived on the morning stage moved out to stand beside him. Soon others began to crowd around. Fargo pushed himself away from the porch post and let Emma help him off the porch and down the street until they were both close enough to hear what was going on.

The old Apache, his face resembling ancient leather, his white hair blowing like cotton in the hot wind, was speaking: ". . . to take back our dead braves. That is why we come. Their bones must rest alongside the bones of their ancestors. Free then will their spirits be to hunt again in the great sky above."

Whittington was obviously willing to placate the

old Apache. "Hell," he said, "I sure don't see no reason why you can't take your dead back." He looked nervously about him at the growing crowd. "What do you men think?" he called. "That all right with you?"

"Save us buryin' 'em," someone shouted gleefully.

Four or five more onlookers responded, all of them favorable to letting the old chief cart off his dead warriors. Someone suggested they take the manure pile too. A few more similar cracks salted the response, but no one objected.

Whittington turned back to the old Apache and nodded his assent.

With great dignity the Indians dismounted and marched solemnly to the manure pile, slung their dead comrades over their shoulders, and brought them back to their mounts. Then, with the fragrant corpses draped over their ponies' withers, they rode back out of town.

As Fargo and Emma turned to go back to the hotel, the fellow in the white stetson overtook Fargo. He was a broad-chested, powerful man, with white hair and a ruddy face. His mustache was as thick and as white as a walrus tusk, his chin solid. He did not look like a man who lost many arguments.

"I don't believe we've met," he said to Fargo. "My card, sir."

Fargo took the card and read:

STANTON HOLLOWAY
*Agent for Arizona Mining
and Smelting, Inc.*

"Pleased to meet you, Mr. Holloway," Fargo said, handing back the card. "My name is Fargo. How can I help you?"

"I see you are headed back to the hotel. Perhaps we could talk there."

As soon as they reached the porch, Emma saw to it that another chair was brought out for Holloway. Then she vanished inside to give the men privacy. As soon as Fargo and Holloway were comfortable and the pleasantries had been concluded, Holloway reached into a pocket and produced a bright, newly minted silver dollar.

"The hostler said you gave this to him when you rode in last night."

Without comment, Fargo nodded.

"Do you mind telling me where you got it?"

"You know where I got it."

"From a newly minted shipment that never reached its destination."

Fargo saw no reason to dispute the man.

"This is most embarrassing for my company, Mr. Fargo. We were hoping to open a mint in Arizona to compete with the one in California. This misadventure has put us in a bad light. Our first batch of minted coins has been a complete loss, unless we can retrieve it."

"What do you want me to do?"

"I have a proposition, Mr. Fargo."

"I'm listening."

Emma came out carrying a tray with two tall glasses of spiked lemonade. They thanked her and she went back inside.

Holloway sipped the cool drink and smiled, delighted

at the extra bite Emma had given the drink. Leaning back, he told Fargo his company's proposition: for the return of the shipment to Holloway, he was authorized to offer Fargo one-tenth of its value.

Fargo's eyebrows canted. "One-tenth? And what do you think that would amount to, offhand?"

"Two thousand dollars, and that is not offhand."

"I don't want the money, Holloway. But I know where that much will do some good."

"Then you accept?"

"Depends. I'll want that offer in writing and signed by you."

"Done." Holloway smiled and sipped on his drink. "Tell me, how soon can you go after the silver?"

"I'll be ready to ride out first thing in the morning."

Holloway nodded, pleased. Then he finished his lemonade and stood up. "Thank you, Mr. Fargo. It is a pleasure doing business with you."

"Likewise," said Fargo.

Fargo watched Holloway heading down the street toward the Express Office, then pushed himself wearily to his feet and limped inside to get out of the heat. If Emma Poole would let him, he would like to take a nap.

He had a long ride ahead of him tomorrow.

The next morning, as Fargo finished loading two casks of black powder and a large coil of Bickford fuse onto the pack horse he'd rented, Holloway appeared.

"You goin' mining, Fargo?"

"You might say that." Favoring his left thigh, Fargo swung gingerly up into his saddle.

"I have that agreement you wanted," Holloway said, handing up a sealed envelope to him.

Reaching down, Fargo took the envelope, opened it, and read the agreement he found inside. It was a clear, legal statement of the deal they had consummated the day before, signed by Stanton Holloway. Tucking the envelope into one of his saddlebags, Fargo nodded his acceptance to Holloway.

"There's just one thing more," Holloway said.

"And what might that be?"

"I want to go with you."

Fargo looked at the man carefully. Holloway stared unblinkingly up at him. He was wearing a well-kept, pearl-handled Colt and there was much about the solidly built agent to convince Fargo he knew how to use it.

"You might have to skip over some singing lead," Fargo warned.

Holloway smiled suddenly. "Been doin' that most of my life."

"Get your horse, then."

It took three days for Fargo and Holloway to reach the valley. They went by way of Carswell's ranch and had found the place deserted, with the exception of the old Indian housekeeper and their wrangler, a stove-up cowpoke who was drunk out of his mind inside the barn.

The wrangler gave them no trouble and told them that Carswell and his two sons, along with the sheriff, his deputy, and three others had ridden out the day before. As Fargo and Holloway mounted up and took out after them, the Indian housekeeper fired futilely after them with an ancient shotgun, the force of its recoil slapping her back through the open doorway.

They followed Carswell's tracks across the Superstitions and arrived at the Papago valley late in the afternoon. Careful to approach from the top of the escarpment, Fargo and Holloway dismounted and peered over. The valley was quiet—too quiet.

Fargo saw no Indian women moving about the village, no men trudging in from the fields. And no fires curling up from their conical lodges. Even the burros seemed to have vanished.

"Over there," Holloway said, pointing.

Fargo followed the man's finger and saw the barely visible body of an Indian sprawled in the brush halfway down the slope well off to the right beyond the escarpment. Looking more closely then, Fargo saw, about twenty yards farther down the slope, another sprawled Papago brave—this one spread-eagle, faceup. There was no question in either man's mind that the two Indians were dead, and there were undoubtedly many more other dead Indians lying about.

From where they were, Fargo could not see Carlotta's adobe house at the other end of the village. Remounting, he and Holloway followed the rim until the adobe building was in full view. Crouching on the rim, they watched.

Three of Carswell's men had herded the men and women of the tribe into and just in front of the adobe building. Sullen in defeat, the Papagos were squatting, others standing, their heads down. It was clear what had happened. Despite Dano's preparations and brave talk, Carswell and his men had simply swept down on them without warning, their superior firepower enough to overcome the Papago Indians' resistance.

Now, while Carswell went looking for the treasure, his men were guarding the rest of the tribe. Fargo swore softly, bitterly, to himself. He wondered how many Papago Indians Carswell and his men had killed. And what about Carlotta?

Pulling back from the ridge, Fargo found a stand of thick juniper. There, he and Holloway tethered the horses.

"You want to stay here and guard these mounts?" Fargo asked Holloway.

"Not on your life."

"Then, come with me."

"What's your plan?"

"First things first. We've got to find Carswell."

"You mean he's not near that adobe building?"

"I didn't see him."

"You got any idea where he might be?"

Fargo nodded. He had a damn good idea. But he had to make sure. "Follow me."

With a shrug, Holloway did as Fargo said.

They ran along the top of the ridge until it crumpled and became part of a series of gullies and hills. Scrambling down one steep gully, they followed it until they came to a series of foothills covered with pine and cottonwoods. They kept on into the cottonwoods, and before long, Fargo was looking down at the adobe house Carlotta's father had built for himself and his Papago bride.

Five lathered horses were tethered to trees in front of it. Fargo pulled up and crouched behind a cottonwood. Holloway pulled up alongside of him, his Colt drawn.

"Carswell's in there?" Holloway asked.

"That's what I figure."

But he wasn't alone, Fargo knew. Carlotta was in there too—and maybe Dano or Pepito. It was one sure way of finding out how to get to the silver and the rest of the treasure. Carswell would simply beat the information out of them.

Fargo heard a high, piercing scream. It went on for a moment or two, then died off. Fargo felt the hair rise on the back of his neck.

Carlotta!

They were working on her and letting Dano or Pepito watch, maybe. When the Indians had had enough, they'd tell Carswell all he needed to know. Maybe. They were, after all, still Indians, brought up not to give in easily.

"Let's go," said Fargo, moving out from behind the tree.

Before they had gone more than fifty yards, Carswell boiled out of the house with his two sons. Ducking behind some brush, Fargo watched as Billy Joe pushed Pepito ahead of him. Pepito's bloodied head was sagging forward and he was barely able to stay on his feet, forcing Billy Joe to heave him up onto his horse, then mount up behind him.

When they galloped off down the slope through the cottonwoods, they left behind two horses, which meant two of Carswell's men were still inside guarding Carlotta.

Slipping swiftly through the trees, Fargo reached the back of the adobe house and peered through a ground-floor window. The kitchen was empty. With Holloway behind him, he moved cautiously along the wall until he reached the back door. A lift latch was all that held it shut.

"Get back," Fargo told Holloway.

Holloway cocked his revolver, a grim set to his mouth.

Lifting his boot, Fargo stomped on the latch, then hurled his shoulder against the door. It gave suddenly and swung wide, catapulting Fargo into the house. As the door swung all the way around and slammed to a halt against the wall, Sheriff Hammond appeared in the kitchen doorway and started to claw for his gun.

"Don't!" Fargo told him.

The sheriff was too stupid to obey. As his fist closed about his gun butt, Fargo fired, catching Hammond in the chest and knocking him back against the stairway. Fargo charged over the sprawled body, Holloway on his heels, and charged up the stairs to the second floor.

The other one was waiting.

His first shot dug into the wall beside Fargo's left ear, momentarily deafening him. Fargo ducked low and waited. The shot had come from a doorway to his left, Carlotta's bedroom. After a moment, Fargo heard Carlotta cry out sharply, as if someone had jabbed her with a sharp instrument.

He cursed and went boiling up the stairs.

At the doorway to Carlotta's bedroom, Fargo came to a sudden, agonized halt. Hammond's deputy was waiting for Fargo with a knife at Carlotta's throat. Blood was already oozing down over her breasts from a sizable nick. She was lying spread-eagled on the bed, her face a mass of purplish bruises, her naked body a pitiful expanse of bloody wounds, as if she had been overrun by a swarm of snakes. Rawhide thongs about her wrists and ankles held her arms and legs outstretched.

And on the floor beyond the bed Fargo saw Dano's naked, crumpled body. Strips of skin hung like raw bacon from his shoulders and back.

"One step, Fargo," said the deputy, "just one step and I'll slit this heathen's throat."

"Do that and you're a dead man."

"My life for hers. Not a bad swap. We all got to go sometime, and I wouldn't mind taking this here bitch with me."

Fargo could barely hear Holloway stealing cautiously up the stairs behind him. The deputy did not appear to be aware of Holloway's presence. Fargo came to a quick decision. Those two shots were likely to bring Carswell or one of his men back to investigate.

The deputy nudged the point of his knife against Carlotta's neck, just above her Adam's apple. Carlotta, her eyes wide in terror, strained to pull her neck back.

"Just let that gun drop to the floor," the deputy told Fargo. "Nice and easy."

Instead, Fargo flung himself forward into the room. As he struck the floor, he fired up at the deputy. His shot went wild, but Holloway stepped calmly into the open doorway and sent two quick slugs into the chest. The man crumpled to the floor beside the bed, his knife dropping from lifeless hands. Fargo got to his feet, kicked the dead man out of his way, and with his bowie sliced through the rawhide binding Carlotta.

"Dano," she whispered hoarsely as she sat up and began rubbing her wrists vigorously. "See to Dano!"

Holloway was already lifting the unconscious Indian from the floor. Ignoring her own bloody wounds, Carlotta jumped up and helped settle Dano onto her bed. Leaning close, she kissed his battered face in a fever of concern, desperately trying to revive him.

Dano's eyelids flickered, then opened. He looked up at her, saw Fargo and Holloway, and almost smiled.

"He'll live," said Fargo.

Only then did Carlotta realize her own battered nakedness. She turned away from Holloway's gaze, blushing suddenly. With a gallant smile, Holloway flipped off the bedsheet and threw it over her.

After introducing Holloway to them, Fargo apologized for not getting there sooner.

"It is not your fault," said Carlotta. "You warned us. But Carswell and his men came upon us with such terrible brutality. Arrows and a few flintlocks are no match for six-guns."

"Do they know how to get to the silver?" Fargo asked.

Carlotta nodded unhappily.

"We did not want to tell them," said Dano, "but when they began on Carlotta . . ."

Fargo looked at Carlotta, frowning. It seemed to him that Dano or Pepito had not given in until Carlotta had endured a considerable amount of punishment. Carlotta caught his look and understood at once what he was thinking.

She shook her head decisively. "You do not understand, Skye," she told him. "They questioned us separately. I was downstairs, bound and gagged, while the men did what they wanted with me. Dano and Pepito were up here with Billy Joe and Carswell. When they took Pepito downstairs to watch what they were doing to me, Pepito could not bear it and promised to take them to the silver."

"Can you two move out now?"

Dano nodded and began to sit up. Fargo winced as he took in Dano's ravaged body. He knew the Indian must be experiencing incredible pain, yet as he pushed himself to a sitting position on the edge of the bed, he did not flinch once.

"First things first," Fargo told them. "Get dressed and we'll ride back into the hills. There's two horses outside you can use. Holloway and I'll be waiting outside in case that shooting brings any of Carswell's men back."

Carlotta nodded, and as Fargo and Holloway hurried from the room, she turned and pulled Dano gently to his feet. There were tears in her eyes as she saw what he had endured—and in Dano's eyes, too, there was pain as he regarded the ravaged body of the woman he loved.

9

Fargo was crouched behind a cottonwood, a rope looped around it. Holloway was across the yard behind a low-lying clump of juniper, holding onto the other end he'd snubbed around a sapling. Fargo had been right. Two gunslicks had been sent to investigate the gunfire and were pushing their mounts to the limit as they pounded their way up the slope.

As they neared the house, the two riders pulled abreast. Waiting until he could count the bullets in each man's gun belt, Fargo lifted the rope off the ground and snapped it taut. So quickly did the two horses go down that it looked as if their legs had been sheared off at the knees. Both riders went hurtling over their heads.

Fargo reached his man first. He had never seen the gunslick before. He was lying dazedly on his back, his hat tumbling away from him, a big army Colt in his right hand. Fargo kicked the gun out of his grasp, then stepped closer and kicked again, catching the man on the point of his unshaven jaw. The fellow flopped over onto his face and lay still, a thin tracery of blood trickling from under his broken face.

Fargo glanced over at Holloway. He apparently had no difficulty either. With the butt of his ivory-handled Colt, he had smashed in the side of his man's head. With the fellow sprawled unconscious at his feet, he straightened and turned to Fargo, the gunslick's Colt stuck in his belt.

"Get the horses," Fargo said as he started back up the slope toward the house.

The back door opened and Carlotta helped Dano out. Fargo gave her a hand with Dano as Holloway brought the sheriff and the deputy's mounts for them. The two horses Fargo and Holloway had sent flying were back on their feet by this time, and the two men mounted them and led the way back up through the cottonwoods, heading for the rim of the escarpment.

Once they reached it, they rode along the rim until Carlotta's house was in view. Dismounting, they peered down at it. This time Fargo saw no crowd of Indians huddled before it. The adobe building and the village appeared deserted.

"There!" Carlotta cried. "See! In the fields."

Glancing up, Fargo saw the tiny figures of Indians fleeing across the fields, heading for the other side of the valley. Carswell must have released them. And why not? He had now what he wanted: a guide to take him to his treasure.

Greatly favoring his left thigh by this time, Fargo hurried back along the rim until he caught sight of Carswell, his two sons, and another man marching toward the base of the cliff. Pepito was leading them.

They were still some distance from the base of the cliff.

Fargo turned to Carlotta. "That other entrance, the one you said led up here, where is it?"

"Back here," she said, turning. "Follow me."

Before long, Carlotta and Dano were standing beside a boulder the width and breadth of a good-sized rain barrel resting on its side. Surrounded by a low, thick cluster of juniper, no one would ever have suspected its presence.

"You mean we have to move that boulder?" Holloway asked.

"Yes," replied Carlotta. "The other entrance to the room is through there."

"I will get lever," Dano said.

He turned and hurried off, returning a moment later with a long thick branch rubbed as smooth as silk and as unyielding as iron. It had apparently served this purpose over the years. Placing one end of the branch in a slight depression under one end of the boulder, Dano began to pry up the boulder. Fargo and Holloway immediately stepped forward to lend a hand. In a matter of minutes, they had manhandled the boulder out of the tunnel entrance.

Leaning close, Fargo could feel a steady, musty breeze as the long-pent air of the cavern below rushed out past him.

"How do you get down?" he asked Carlotta.

"There are steps cut in the rock just below this opening. They lead down to a narrow tunnel that will take you to the treasure room."

Fargo saw the sudden wariness on Holloway's face. "You mean I have to go down there to get that silver?"

"Unless you want to wait up here, where it'll be a lot safer."

The big man shrugged. "Hell, no sense in letting you have all the fun. Let's go."

"Appreciate it, Holloway. But first I got something to take with me." He looked at Carlotta and Dano. "Get back to the rim. Let me know how Carswell's doing. I want to know when he starts climbing up that ladder to the main cavern."

As Carlotta and Dano hurried off, Fargo and Holloway went back to the spot where they had tethered their mounts. Unloading the black powder from his pack horse, he handed one keg to Holloway, took the other along with the saddlebag containing the Bickford fuse, his drills and hammer, and led the way back to the tunnel entrance.

Putting his keg on the ground beside the tunnel entrance, Fargo asked Holloway for the gun he had taken from the gunslick, then left Holloway and hurried over to Carlotta and Dano.

"They've reached the base of the cliff," Carlotta said. "Pepito is climbing up to get the rope ladder."

"Are Orzoko and Tamio still on guard?"

Dano shrugged unhappily. "I am not sure."

"Stay here," Fargo told them, handing Dano the gun he had just taken from Holloway. "Guard this here entrance. Holloway and I are going down now to get the silver."

When Fargo arrived back at the tunnel entrance, Holloway cocked an eyebrow. "Would you like to tell me what in hell you're up to with all this black powder?"

"It's a long story. If we get out of this in one piece, I'll explain the whole thing to you."

"That's a promise?"

"You have my word."

Holloway looked at Fargo for a long moment, then shrugged and eased himself down into the tunnel.

"Watch out for scorpions," Fargo called softly.

Holloway glanced up at him and for a moment Fargo thought the man was going to tell him to shove the entire operation up his ass. Instead, he reached back for one of the two kegs. Fargo handed it to him, then followed after him, carrying the remaining keg and the saddlebag.

"Fargo!" Carlotta called down to him.

"What?"

"There are torches on the wall—before you start down."

"Thanks."

From the light filtering down from the entrance behind him, Fargo glimpsed Holloway disappearing around a bend in the tunnel ahead of him. A moment later, Fargo followed after him and was plunged into a darkness so profound that he pulled up sharply before moving on. The slip into hell must be like this, he thought. Reaching out, he felt along the wall. His hand struck the handle of a torch. He lifted it out of its niche, scratched a sulfur match to life along the wall, and held it to the tip. The torch blazed smokily, then cleared somewhat, and Fargo saw Holloway disappearing ahead of him down a narrow, winding passageway.

The smoke from the torch caused his eyes to smart, even though he kept it as high over his head as he could while he wound deeper and deeper into the cliff's bowels. At last he saw Holloway disappear ahead of him through a low opening. A moment later Fargo followed after him into the treasure room.

Holloway was standing beside the keg of black powder, looking back at Fargo as he approached with the torch.

"Look behind you, Holloway," Fargo said, holding his torch high over both their heads.

Holloway spun around and in that instant saw the extent of the gleaming riches that materialized out of the darkness. For a moment he was speechless as he took it all in. Then he turned to Fargo. "My God, Fargo," he gasped. "This—this is incredible, beyond belief!"

"Now you know what Carswell's really after."

His voice hushed, Holloway said, "I don't wonder."

"Your silver's over there," Fargo said, indicating the three sacks of silver coins in the corner. "Start hauling them topside. I got other business. And hustle your ass. We don't have much time."

Fargo found another torch, lit it, and stuck it in the wall alongside the torch he had brought down with him. Then he placed one of the kegs down beside the main entrance to the cavern and the other one just inside the secret entrance. By the time he had finished drilling the few powder holes he judged necessary and then measuring out the sections of Bickford fuse, Holloway had returned for the second of the three sacks of silver.

He was disappearing with the third one when Fargo heard movement in the tunnel outside the door. Holloway heard it also and held up.

"Keep going," Fargo whispered. "I'll handle this myself."

Holloway was about to protest, but Fargo waved him on. He shrugged and disappeared up the steep, winding tunnel. Fargo lifted down the two torches, stomped them out, then flung them into a far corner so their fumes would not alert Carswell. In the sudden Stygian darkness, Fargo took out his Colt and his bowie and moved back into a recessed corner he had already selected well to the right of the door.

Then he waited.

Fargo heard the lock being opened, the bolt thrown. The door swung back. Light from several torches flooded into the room. Pepito entered first, stumbling, as someone shoved him roughly in. Catching himself, the Indian vanished into the darkness on the other side of the door. Then came a bearded gunslick, followed by Billy Joe and Seth. Seth was carrying a torch, holding it high and staring in amazed disbelief at the heaped treasure glittering in its flickering light. Billy Joe and the gunman, too, stared in stunned wonderment. Carswell entered finally. He too was carrying a torch.

"Well now, lads," he said, his voice rumbling in triumph, "was I tellin' you the truth or was I just beatin' on my gums?"

"Pa," cried Seth, "I can't believe it!"

Billy Joe ripped off his hat and slapped his thigh with it. "We're rich," he cried.

"Rich?" Carswell echoed. "It's more than that, you jackass!"

"What do you mean, Pa?"

"I mean we got enough here to ransom a country."

The gunslick turned to Carswell, his eyes gleaming greedily. "Jesus Christ, Carswell," he said ferverently. "I sure do thank you for letting me in on this."

Carswell chuckled, lifting his six-gun, and shot the man calmly between the eyes.

As the man crashed back onto a pile of gleaming goblets and silverware, Carswell calmly holstered his weapon.

"I hate them as take things for granted," he told Seth and Billy Joe. "I never told Harry I was goin' to let him in on this."

Seth glanced nervously down at the dead gunslick, then at his father. "Pa, you didn't need to do that. There's plenty here for all of us."

"You want some of that same medicine, Seth?"

"No, Pa," Seth said meekly.

Billy Joe had already forgotten about their dead confederate as he strode out into the pile of treasure, reaching down eagerly to bring up first one, then another glittering trinket, each one tossed aside in turn as he espied other, more glittering treasures. He found a gold and ruby necklace, but then reached over to pull free a gold scabbard with a silver-handled sword resting in it. The hilt was festooned with precious gems, including rubies and emeralds. Crying out in delight, Billy Joe dropped the necklace and withdrew the sword from the gold scabbard.

"Look, Pa," he cried, flashing the sword over his head.

And that was when he saw Fargo.

He dropped the sword and pointed.

Seth and Carswell swung around as Fargo stepped out of the shadows, his Colt leveled on them.

"Pepito," Fargo called, "get out of here!"

Pepito materialized out of the darkness where he had been crouched and scrambled quickly past the three Carswells. A moment later he had vanished back out through the door.

"Well, now," drawled Carswell, "I must admit, Fargo, you're as troublesome and persistent as a horsefly in August."

"But a mite more deadly."

"Now, don't tell me you still hold a grudge."

"That what you call it?"

"Think a moment, Fargo. There's enough here for all of us. You'll be rich, richer than Croesus! Think of the big hotels, cigars, women. Why, man, it's all here, waiting for you!"

Fargo smiled. "Waiting for me—like it was for that poor son of a bitch you just gunned down a minute ago. You're a Carswell, all right. Next to you, a mad dog is a minor nuisance."

"You ain't makin' sense, Fargo. I told you. I'm willing to share." He turned to his sons. "Ain't that the truth, Seth, Billy Joe?"

"Sure thing, Pa," said Billy Joe.

Seth just nodded, his eyes on the big muzzle of Fargo's Colt.

"Well, then, I got some good news for you," Fargo told them. "You three won't have to share this here treasure with anyone."

Carswell frowned. "How's that, Fargo?" He was aware Fargo had a kicker coming.

"You heard me. You appreciate this treasure so much, you worked so hard to get, I don't see why you can't just stay here and enjoy it."

"Stay here?" Billy Joe echoed nervously.

"That's right," Fargo said, looking straight at Carswell's straw-haired son. "Until your bones turn to dust."

Seth moistened dry lips. "Jesus, Fargo, what're you sayin'?"

"Turn around, all three of you. Slowly."

But Seth didn't want to die. With a sudden cry, he flung his torch at Fargo. At the same time, Carswell, dropping his torch, drew his Colt and fired. Seth's torch sailed past Fargo's right shoulder and Carswell's slug whined off the rock wall behind him. Dropping to one knee, Fargo returned Carswell's fire. He missed, the slug ricocheting into the pile of treasure, slamming a jeweled box into icy fragments. By then there was little light as the torches guttered feebly on the floor, and before Fargo could fire again, Carswell and his two sons flung themselves around and darted out of the room.

Fargo stood up and placed the torches back into the walls. In a moment they were spreading a flickering light over the cavern. Fargo went to the door then and heard the three pounding toward the tunnel leading back the way they had come. A grim smile on his face, he pulled shut the door. They would never get back out through that wall, he knew. Only Pepito's educated hands could manage such a miracle. Meanwhile, Fargo had a few more details to attend to—black powder to be tamped into the holes he had drilled and, after that, lengths of Bickford fuse to play out.

He worked swiftly in the dim light, moving about so much that he broke open his thigh wound. At last, as he was getting ready to follow after Holloway, he heard cautious footsteps approaching the door. Reaching up, he flung the torches across the cavern, plunging the place into a flickering darkness. Crouching by the escape tunnel, Fargo saw the door open a crack, then wider. A moment later the three desperate men peered in.

Fargo flung a shot at them and they vanished back out the doorway, pushing the door shut.

"Fargo," Carswell cried through the door. "We can't get out! We're trapped. You're trapped, too!"

"No, I'm not, Carswell."

"What do you mean?"

"Just what I said."

There was a silence. Fargo could hear the three of them arguing frantically.

Then Carswell's voice came again. "You can't leave us here!"

"Oh, yes, I can."

"For the love of God, Fargo!"

"Yes, Carswell. For the love of God!"

Fargo lit his spitter, the short length of Bickford fuse he needed to light the longer fuses, then held it to the first of the fuses he had already split in readiness, the one leading to the charge he had planted about the cavern's doorway. The fuse caught instantly.

Fargo knew that a Bickford fuse burned almost exactly one foot in thirty seconds. Counting to himself, he turned and limped up the steep tunnel. When he came to the second fuse, he paused only long enough to light it also. As he reached the last turn in the passageway, he finished counting and flinched, waiting for the first explosion. When it came, he thought his eardrums had burst. Then he fired the last fuse.

turned the corner, and a moment later climbed out of the tunnel.

It was close to dusk, and never had a sky, already gleaming with stars, looked so good to him.

But he didn't have time to enjoy it.

"Get back," he called out to Carlotta and Dano, who were rushing toward him. Behind them, Holloway was standing by his horse.

"What's going on?" Carlotta cried. "I heard an explosion!"

"Is Pepito out?"

"Yes," Carlotta told him. "We just saw him climbing down the ladder."

Fargo smiled, immensely relieved.

At that moment the ground shook under him. It was not enough to cause him to fall, but it was the final blast he was worried about, since it was so close to the surface.

Limping painfully by this time, he herded Carlotta and Dano ahead of him for about fifteen yards when the last of his charges detonated. The ground erupted, showering them all with debris. Fargo staggered forward, almost losing his balance. Hunching his shoulders against the showering debris, he turned and looked back.

The junipers at the tunnel entrance had sunken into the ground and the boulder that covered the entrance had vanished. What remained was a slight indentation in the ground, most of it covered with fresh soil. Soon, Fargo knew, weeds and then grass would cover it. The junipers would grow up around the spot once more, only this time there would be no boulder hidden in its midst.

The fabled treasure of the Hohokam was locked forever in the bowels of this mountain, while the bones of four dead men would serve as guardians down through the centuries.

A week later, the wound in his thigh almost completely healed, Fargo dismounted in front of Tularo's livery and led his pinto inside. When he came out, slapping the dust off his buckskins with his hat, he glanced across the street toward the Arizona House and saw Stanton Holloway stride out onto the porch, a cheroot in his mouth.

Fargo had intended to cross directly to the saloon, eager to wash Arizona's landscape off his tonsils. But when Holloway waved to him, Fargo decided he might as well join him. As he recalled, Emma Poole fixed excellent lemonade.

Mounting the porch steps, Fargo swept off his hat and mopped his brow. "See you got back here, all right, Holloway."

"Yup. A small party of Apaches hurried me on my way, but I made it without incident. You got here just in time. My stage is pulling out within the hour."

Fargo slumped into the white wicker chair beside Holloway and let his body sink into its familiar contours There was a tall glass of lemonade on the table between them. Fargo heard footsteps approaching the hotel door and glanced around in time to see Emma stride out onto the porch.

"Fargo, I thought I heard your voice!"

"I'm parched, Emma. Would you be nice enough to make another lemonade—and leave the pitcher here."

She laughed and vanished back inside.

"Fargo," Holloway began, "you promised you'd explain why you blew up that cavern, burying all that wealth inside—not to mention the Carswells. Now I'd like to hear it."

Fargo took a deep breath and, without asking, sipped a little of Holloway's drink. "Holloway, do you know what happened to Sutter when they found gold on his land?"

Holloway nodded. "He lost everything."

"That's right. The world stampeded in, and before you knew it, California was a state. Ever think of what happened to the Spanish who owned land there?"

"They lost it."

"Almost every acre. They became outcasts in their own land."

Holloway frowned thoughtfully. "I see. Yes, it makes sense now, what you did. Once word got out about that treasure, those Indians would have lost the valley in the rush that was bound to follow."

"And while that treasure was there," Fargo pointed out, "they would always have the threat of more Carswells or Apaches eager to loot that room. It would be a never-ending source of trouble. And sooner or later, the word *would* get out, just as it did this last time."

"Yes, I see," Holloway said, finishing up. "Now, all those Indians have got is that silver you gave them and their land. And as long as they keep their noses clean, that's all they'll ever need."

Fargo nodded in agreement.

"And you squared your account with Carswell."

"Yes."

Emma appeared with his lemonade and the full

pitcher he had requested. Placing it down on the table, she held her face close to his for a moment. "Your bath is ready," she whispered.

He smiled, grateful. "I'll be right up."

As Emma disappeared back into the hotel, Fargo poured himself a drink and downed it, feeling better at once. Holloway's stage rolled past the hotel, heading for the Express Office farther down the street.

Holloway sighed and stood up. "I must be leaving now," he said, sticking out his hand. "It was a pleasure, Fargo. I hope we meet again."

Fargo stood up to shake the man's hand. "Likewise."

Holloway went back inside the hotel for his carpetbag. Fargo sat back down and poured himself another drink. A moment later Holloway left the hotel and descended the porch steps. At the foot of them, he turned suddenly.

"Fargo?"

"Yes?"

"You destroyed one entrance—the one we used. What about the other one?"

"I underestimated the charges I laid somewhat. That first blast not only closed off the treasure room, it caused the entire system of tunnels above it to collapse. That sliding wall I told you about leading down toward the cavern will never budge again."

Holloway smiled, obviously pleased at this news, then turned and strode off down the street.

Watching him go, Fargo allowed his thoughts to drift back to the now-peaceful valley he had left a few days before, and to Carlotta and her new husband, Dano. Carlotta had been most relieved when Fargo insisted that Dano was the man her father's spirit had intended she marry, not him, and it was a very happy couple that saw him off, his thigh healed finally, their joy in each other radiating out over the entire valley, it seemed, as they waved good-bye.

Fargo finished his lemonade, got to his feet, and went inside. He was looking forward to that bath Emma had promised him.

When Fargo entered the back room, the steam was heavier than usual, so heavy he had to pause a moment to get his bearings. Then, groping through the wet clouds, he came upon a high-backed bathtub larger than any he had seen before.

Out of the steam, a bucket in hand, strode Emma Poole, stark-maked. "What are you waiting for?" she asked, stepping into the steaming water. "Aren't you going to join me?"

"Both of us?"

"I need a bath, too."

"At the same time?"

"Do you object?"

"Hell, no."

As he stepped in and stood for a moment facing her, he paid scant attention to the near-scalding water lapping his thighs. And neither did Emma. Instead, she was looking up in fascination at what was staring impertinently down at her. Reaching up, she drew Fargo into the searing water and with a soaped sponge began to lave him thoroughly.

All over.

It was a long, delightful bath, and when at last Fargo stood up reluctantly to let Emma towel him off, he felt as light as a feather. He could tell Emma felt the same way. They had both emptied each other out, completely.

He had figured he might stay in Tularo for a few days at the most. He was sick of the murderous sun and the dust. But with this level of accommodations, he just might stay longer—for a week more, at least.

LOOKING FORWARD!

The following is the opening section
from the next novel in the exciting
Trailsman series from Signet:

The Trailsman #45
KILLER CARAVAN

1861 the Kentucky-Tennessee border,
a land where tomorrow's shadows
were cast in today's blood . . .

He had undressed in the still darkness and now he was
at the edge of the bed, staring down at the girl there.

She was pretty.

She was blond.

She was naked.

But she was not the girl he expected to be there.

And she was very dead.

"Shit," Fargo murmured. The sound of footsteps in
the hall outside broke into his frowning thoughts. He
lifted his head as the footsteps grew louder and the
sudden pounding on the door sounded like thunder.

"You in there, open up. This is the sheriff," the
voice shouted.

"Goddamn," Fargo hissed as he swung from the
edge of the bed and started to pull on trousers.

"I said, this is the sheriff. Open up," the voice shouted as the pounding began again.

Fargo looked at the girl in the bed as he buttoned his trousers. She was small-boned, flatish breasts, a thin girl, somehow waiflike even in death. A small gold circle dangled from a thin chain on one wrist. He lifted it and saw the name *Crystal* engraved there.

The pounding on the door commenced again, stronger and louder, and he heard other voices. "Open up in there, Fargo," the sheriff's voice called again, and Fargo felt the frown dig into his brow at the sound of his name. He was jamming his feet into boots as he heard the man's angry shout. "Break the goddamn door in," the sheriff ordered.

Fargo rose, strapped on his gun belt, and scooped up the rest of his clothes as he ran to the window. He looked out and swore silently. No fire escape. Not even a drainpipe to shimmy down. He measured the distance to the ground and cursed again. Two stories were an almost guaranteed broken leg. As he pulled back from the window, he saw two men run around the corner of the building to stare up at the window. The boot slammed into the door and Fargo saw the door almost give way. He slipped his shirt on, jammed his hat on his head as another kick sent splinters flying from the door. One more kick would do it, he knew. He pushed aside the thoughts and the anger that churned inside him. There was no time for anything but getting out, now.

He drew the big Colt from its holster as he crossed the room in three long-legged strides. He flattened himself with his back to the wall beside the door as another kick sent the latch splintering aside. The door flew open and the three men rushed in. Fargo's leg shot out, caught the first one around the ankles, and he saw the man go down. The other two rushing after him went sprawling over him, and Fargo spun, starting to race out the open door. He glanced back and caught the glint of the five-pointed star of the third man's shirt as the sheriff started to push himself to his feet. Fargo raced down the hallway and took the flight of steps three at a time. He reached the last step just as the figure appeared in front of him to block his path. As he saw the man go for his gun, he leapt, swinging out with a long, looping right as he did so. The blow hit with the force of his diving leap behind it, and the man went down, the gun just out of its holster firing wildly into the wall of the stairway.

Fargo let his boot land in the man's stomach as he ran past him, the other figures pounding down the stairs after him. He streaked for the door of the hotel and ran outside into the night. Flicking the reins of the pinto from the hitching post, he vaulted onto the horse's back. The two figures ran around the corner of the building just as he wheeled the horse. He let two shots fly at them, saw both figures dive to safety as he sent the powerful Ovaro into a full gallop down the darkened main street of town. He raced in a straight path for a few minutes, then sent the horse veering through an opening between a granary and a warehouse, came out at the back side of the buildings, and raced for the deep timber that bordered the town.

He reined up for a moment, listened, and heard shouts and the sound of hoofbeats racing along Main Street. He sent the Ovaro forward again, a trot, this time, and disappeared into the thickness of the timber. He rode deeper into the forest until the foliage grew so heavy it shut out all but a flicker of moonlight and turned the world into a still and stygian place. He halted then, slid to the ground, and drew a deep breath. Slowly, he lowered himself to the ground, rested against the trunk of a thick sycamore, and let everything that had happened so quickly and so unexpectedly flood back over him.

The surge of anger came first. It had been a damn trap. No mistake, no wrong room. They'd known he was in there. They'd called his name, and that might have been a mistake on the sheriff's part. But they had known, tried to trap him in the room with a dead girl. It wasn't hard to figure their next move, to accuse him of killing her. A perfect frame-up, neat and simple. And it had almost worked for them. Only none of it made any damn sense. The frown dug deep into his brow as he rested his head back against the tree trunk. He'd start at the beginning, go over everything that had happened since he'd hit town the day before. He'd relive it step by step. Maybe something would offer an answer, or at least a clue. He closed his eyes and let his thoughts wind backward.

He'd reached Hawk Ridge yesterday afternoon, bringing in a hundred head of prime Texas longhorn. He'd taken the herd through the Apache and Choctaw and past the Shawnee, from the dry heat of the Texas

Territory into the damp heat of Arkansas, across the Mississipi and the Tennessee and a hatful of lesser rivers, a trail never taken before by anyone. The Calloon brothers had hired him to prove that Texas beef could be brought as far north as the Kentucky border in a reasonable amount of time. But there'd been something more than a possible business venture behind it, Fargo recalled. When he led the first of the herd into Hawk Ridge, he'd been met not just by the Calloon brothers but by a delegation of town officials.

The celebration that followed and went into the night also seemed almost an official town celebration. But a lot of good Tennessee sipping whiskey had flowed and he'd had his share. Hawk Ridge was a prospering town, he'd taken note, astride the Kentucky-Tennessee border and sitting at the gateway to the best route down across Tennessee and into Alabama and Georgia. But when the celebrating came to an end, he'd gone to enjoy the luxury of a good soft bed at the town's only hotel, a place called the Traveler's House. He'd slept soundly, fatigue and the whiskey combining to assure that, and woke hungry with the morning.

There'd been nothing untoward or in any way odd about the events following his arrival. But then the morning had brought him to Aimee. He'd gone downstairs for coffee and biscuits in a small dining room off the slightly seedy lobby. She was the only person there beside himself, slowly sipping coffee, dark-blond hair pulled back in a bun, good, even features, blue eyes under eyebrows that matched her hair. She wore a dark-blue cotton shirt and a black skirt and he saw modest breasts that nonetheless curved the shirt outward with a nice, upward line. She smiled, a bright smile that was tinged with a hint of private amusement.

"Aimee Taylor," she said. "You're the one who brought the herd in yesterday."

"Guilty." He smiled.

She gestured to a chair at the small table. "Please join me," she said. "I got in yesterday, too, though no one gave me the attention they did you." She laughed, a nice, soft sound.

"Don't know why. You're a damn sight prettier than I am," Fargo offered.

"But I'm not famous. I'm not the Trailsman." She laughed, and her eyes danced over the rim of the coffeecup at him, appraising, studying. "I heard some of the men talking about you," Aimee Taylor said.

"Don't believe everything you hear," Fargo answered.

"I don't, usually, but in this case I think I will." Aimee laughed, leaned back, and he watched the cotton blouse grow beautifully tight across the twin curves of her breasts. She was, he decided, a very attractive young woman, an almost mischievous quality to her.

"What's brought you to Hawk Ridge?" he asked as an elderly black man in a frayed jacket brought coffee and biscuits.

"Came with my aunt, all the way from Boston. She's still asleep in our room. She wants to get as much sleep as she can before she leaves on the midnight stage to Pine Bludd," Aimee Taylor said.

"But you're staying?" Fargo queried.

"Yes, for a while, at least. I'm wondering about starting a business here. A relative left me some money," she said.

"A woman setting up a business?" Fargo frowned.

Her smile held a touch of tolerance. "You think the only business a woman can go into is a dance hall?" she returned.

"No, I didn't mean that, and you're not the dance-hall type. I was just a little surprised. Most women don't start up their own business."

"They do back in Boston," Aimee Taylor answered. "But I suppose that's one of the things I'll have to think about down here. Are you staying on?"

"Just long enough to pick up my paycheck at the bank this afternoon," he answered.

She let a tiny pout touch her lips. "I'm disappointed. I was hoping to get to know you better," she said. "It seems you've a reputation for more than trailbreaking."

"You've done a lot of listening," he said.

"Maybe," she said, suddenly wary, but the frank interest stayed in the blue eyes and her lower lip had dropped open a fraction and the tip of her tongue showed for an instant.

He smiled inwardly. He'd seen it happen before, women fascinated by hearing that a man was an especially good lover. Maybe it was a kind of challenge or maybe the attraction of playing with danger. He didn't know and didn't much care, but it happened and he fastened Aimee Taylor with his lake-blue eyes.

"That excites you?" he slid at her.

"Let's say it makes you more interesting," she answered. "Look, I'm going to rent a horse at the stable. I want to look over the country around here. I'd be honored to have the Trailsman ride with me," she said. She had a way of wrapping everything she said with a hint of something more.

He smiled. "Why, not? I've plenty of time."

Aimee Taylor rose and he saw she was taller than she'd seemed seated, a long waist and nice hips. "Meet me at the stable," she said with a quick, bright smile.

He nodded, watched her leave. She walked the way she talked, no flaunting, no broad sway of her hips, just a little wriggle that hinted at something more. He left a coin on the table and walked from the hotel. Outside, a dozen black men loaded lengths of two-by-fours onto a hickory-built lumber wagon with the over-size rear wheels, and he was reminded that this was a state where a different rule of life held sway.

He halted at the Ovaro, untied the horse, and led the magnificently striking animal down to the stable. Aimee appeared on a dapple-gray gelding. He swung onto the Ovaro and she fell in alongside him as he rode from town.

Once on the road outside town, he put his horse into a canter and halted when he crested a hill thick with white ash and gambel oak. He gestured to the rise of thick, green mountains to the north over the border into Kentucky. "The Cumberland Range," he told Aimee Taylor. "Rugged, dense mountain forest, all of it. But ahead of you, down that way, that's the Cumberland Plateau. It cuts right through Tennessee to the south, the golden route. On the east over there are the Great Smokies. This is rich country, good farming land where it's level enough, good logging country in the mountains. Lots of folks settle here. Lots more travel on through."

"I don't expect to become either a farmer or a logger," Aimee said.

"What do you figure on starting?" Fargo asked.

"Maybe a dry-goods store, especially for women's things," she said. "A place women could buy goods for the trip south or for settling down." She moved her dapple-gray forward. "Show me some more of the countryside," she said.

He took her partway into the start of the Cumberland Plateau and up to the edge of Norris Lake. The sun had slipped into the afternoon sky when she halted atop a low hill that looked over the sparkling blue lake waters, slid from the horse, and stretched out on the ground. "It's beautiful here," she said.

Fargo dismounted and sat down beside her. "You're beautiful here," he said.

Aimee Taylor's little smile was made of quiet confidence. "You sure you wouldn't consider staying around?" she asked.

He half-shrugged. "I might, if I had good-enough reason to stay a spell," he answered. "You ask me out riding for that?"

"Not really," she said, and leaned back on her elbows. Her breasts pushed hard against the dark-blue cotton shirt.

"You're putting a strain on my good manners," Fargo remarked. "On purpose, I'm thinking."

She laughed. "Maybe," she allowed.

He leaned toward her. "I don't like to strain myself," he said as he brought his lips to hers.

She returned his kiss at once, her lips soft, warmly resilient, and he felt her mouth draw open, the tip of her tongue dart out to touch his and withdraw at once. His hand found the top of the neckline on the cotton blouse, slid under the collar, moved up to one smooth, round shoulder. Her lips parted again for him and he pressed into their warmth as his hand moved from her shoulder, crept along the collarbone, moved down. He felt the buttons of the blouse come open. The neckline fell away and his fingers moved lightly, quickly, over the swell of one soft breast. He felt her quiver, shudder, and her hands tightened against him. He wondered if she were really taken with him, hungry or just easy. But he never looked a gift horse in the mouth. Or a gift beaver.

His mouth stayed on hers as he slid his hand lower, let his fingers move across the tiny tip, cup the soft roundness in his palm, and he heard Aimee Taylor gasp out. "Oh, so nice . . . oh, my God." He let his thumb caress the tiny tip, used his wrist to push the blouse open altogether, and heard her tiny gasped breaths. Her legs rose, together, and her pelvis twisted and she pushed against him, tore herself from his hand to sit up. She pulled the blouse over her breasts at once as her eyes met his, suddenly dark and deep with desire fought down.

"No, not here. I can't here," she said.

"It's great under a warm sun," he told her, reaching one hand to her.

She shook her head vigorously. "No, I can't. I'd always be afraid someone might be watching. I'd hate that," she said. She leaned forward, took his hand impulsively. "I can't out here, I just can't," she said.

"Sorry," he said.

"No, tonight, in my room at the Travelers's House," Aimee said. "It'd be different there. It'd be fine there."

"When?" he asked.

"My aunt will get the stage by eleven-thirty," Aimee Taylor said as she buttoned her blouse. "Midnight in my room. I'll be back by then, waiting for you. I'll leave the door open," she said, her eyes full of dark lights. "Room Five B."

"Midnight," he said, and cast a glance at the sky. "I'll just have time to get to the bank in town before they close."

"Then we'll hurry," she said, and quickly pulled herself onto the dapple-gray.

He rode back toward Hawk Ridge at a fast trot, not unhappy with the way the day had gone. Paycheck first, pussy later. It was a world of unexpected rewards, sometimes.

Aimee chattered brightly as they rode, mostly about her ideas for opening a shop. But when he halted before the bank, her eyes were deep and round and full of dark turbulence again. "Midnight," she breathed. "You will come, won't you?"

"In every way." He grinned, watched her ride on, and then went into the bank. The check was waiting for him and he folded it into his saddlebag when he returned to the Ovaro. He wound his way to the big corral just outside town, where the Calloon brothers had put the herd, and had a drink with Bert Calloon as it grew dark. He rode back through town, let the pinto go at a slow walk. The dance hall sat smack in the center of town and spewed a square of light, noise, and smoke into the street. A girl in a green silk dress two sizes too small for her lounged outside, and he saw her eyes watch him as he approached. He glanced up at the sign over the doorway, the red letters bright even in the dark. BIG BELLE'S PLACE, they proclaimed. He returned his gaze to the girl, false eyelashes, painted nails, too much rouge, and junk jewelry hanging from her right wrist. He rode on and saw the mixture of disappointment and resignation in her face.

He halted under the low-spreading branches of a big box elder just beyond town and stretched out on the ground, let himself half-doze until he saw the moon nearing the midnight sky. He climbed onto the Ovaro and cantered back to Hawk Ridge, the town grown dark and still except for the dance hall.

At the Traveler's House an elderly man looked up from the desk as he passed and went up the stairs to the second floor. The room was at the end of a narrow hallway, and he felt the pleasant glow of anticipation stir inside him. His hand closed around the doorknob and he turned the knob. The door opened at once and he smiled. Aimee had been true to her word. He stepped inside the room, closed the door behind him, and heard the latch snap on. He blinked for a moment in the darkness of the room. A dim light from the lone window on the other side of the room outlined the figure atop the bed, just enough for him to see she lay naked and waiting. He started to pull off clothes as he crossed the room, gun belt first, then shirt, trousers next.

He was naked when he reached her—naked and surprised as all hell.

Fargo snapped his eyes open and his thoughts stopped unwinding. He sat straight and his lips pulled back in distaste. He'd gone back over everything, moment by moment, recreating each incident. But nothing offered so much as a hint, much less a clue or an answer. He stared into the night as he pulled on his thoughts again. The girl outside the dance hall flashed through his mind, but he couldn't find a reason for it. He squinted, saw her standing outside Big Belle's Place as he'd ridden by, and he swore under his breath. She meant nothing, yet she clung in his mind. He put the image of her aside.

But there was one thing that was certain beyond all doubt: Aimee Taylor had set him up and baited the trap. It had been planned and very smoothly executed. But why? And who did it? A sheriff had been there. Was he part of it, or had he just been pointed in the right direction? Fargo felt the spiral of cold rage push aside bewilderment. Somebody had tried to set him up for a murder charge and he couldn't exclude Aimee Taylor. Maybe she had been more than just lure and bait. The question leapt in his mind again. Why? Why any of it?

He pushed himself to his feet to gaze into the night toward Hawk Ridge. The first step was to find a lying, sweet-talking little bitch named Aimee Taylor. But he'd be foolhardy to ride back now. They'd still be searching. Maybe the sheriff had posted guards in the room just in case he did return. Besides, there'd be little to find out now. He had to wait till morning, when people would be up and around to question. He drew a deep breath and stretched out under the box elder again. Before he closed his eyes, the frail, waiflike girl naked in the bed swam into his thoughts. There had been no gunshot or knife wounds on her. Slow strangulation would have left her unmarked. Or an overdose of Tansy.

The name of her bracelet had said Crystal. An oversight on somebody's part to leave it on her. Had she been killed just to set him up? If so, he was dealing with a murderously cold and ruthless bastard. Aimee Taylor came into his thoughts, and he felt himself frown. He couldn't see that kind of venomous ruthlessness in her. But then he'd learned never to underestimate the female of the species. But he was going to find out, goddammit, he swore, for himself and for a poor waiflike little girl named Crystal. Somebody owed her that much.

6 u

Exciting Westerns by Jon Sharpe from SIGNET

(0451)

☐ THE TRAILSMAN #1: SEVEN WAGONS WEST	(127293—$2.50)
☐ THE TRAILSMAN #2: THE HANGING TRAIL	(110536—$2.25)
☐ THE TRAILSMAN #3: MOUNTAIN MAN KILL	(121007—$2.50)
☐ THE TRAILSMAN #4: THE SUNDOWN SEARCHERS	(122003—$2.50)
☐ THE TRAILSMAN #5: THE RIVER RAIDERS	(127188—$2.50)
☐ THE TRAILSMAN #6: DAKOTA WILD	(119886—$2.50)
☐ THE TRAILSMAN #7: WOLF COUNTRY	(123697—$2.50)
☐ THE TRAILSMAN #8: SIX-GUN DRIVE	(121724—$2.50)
☐ THE TRAILSMAN #9: DEAD MAN'S SADDLE	(126629—$2.50)
☐ THE TRAILSMAN #10: SLAVE HUNTER	(114655—$2.25)
☐ THE TRAILSMAN #11: MONTANA MAIDEN	(116321—$2.25)
☐ THE TRAILSMAN #12: CONDOR PASS	(118375—$2.50)
☐ THE TRAILSMAN #13: BLOOD CHASE	(119274—$2.50)
☐ THE TRAILSMAN #14: ARROWHEAD TERRITORY	(120809—$2.50)
☐ THE TRAILSMAN #15: THE STALKING HORSE	(121430—$2.50)
☐ THE TRAILSMAN #16: SAVAGE SHOWDOWN	(122496—$2.50)
☐ THE TRAILSMAN #17: RIDE THE WILD SHADOW	(122801—$2.50)
☐ THE TRAILSMAN #18: CRY THE CHEYENNE	(123433—$2.50)
☐ THE TRAILSMAN #19: SPOON RIVER STUD	(123875—$2.50)
☐ THE TRAILSMAN #20: THE JUDAS KILLER	(124545—$2.50)
☐ THE TRAILSMAN #21: THE WHISKEY GUNS	(124898—$2.50)
☐ THE TRAILSMAN #22: THE BORDER ARROWS	(125207—$2.50)
☐ THE TRAILSMAN #23: THE COMSTOCK KILLERS	(125681—$2.50)
☐ THE TRAILSMAN #24: TWISTED NOOSE	(126203—$2.50)

Prices higher in Canada

Wild Westerns by Warren T. Longtree

SIGNET Westerns You'll Enjoy by Leo P. Kelley

(0451)

☐ CIMARRON #1: CIMARRON AND THE HANGING JUDGE (120582—$2.50)*
☐ CIMARRON #2: CIMARRON RIDES THE OUTLAW TRAIL (120590—$2.50)*
☐ CIMARRON #3: CIMARRON AND THE BORDER BANDITS

(122518—$2.50)*
☐ CIMARRON #4: CIMARRON IN THE CHEROKEE STRIP (123441—$2.50)*
☐ CIMARRON #5: CIMARRON AND THE ELK SOLDIERS (124898—$2.50)*
☐ CIMARRON #6: CIMARRON AND THE BOUNTY HUNTERS

(125703—$2.50)*
☐ CIMARRON #7: CIMARRON AND THE HIGH RIDER (126866—$2.50)*
☐ CIMARRON #8: CIMARRON IN NO MAN'S LAND (128230—$2.50)*
☐ CIMARRON #9: CIMARRON AND THE VIGILANTES (129180—$2.50)*
☐ CIMARRON #10: CIMARRON AND THE MEDICINE WOLVES

(130618—$2.50)*
☐ CIMARRON #11: CIMARRON ON HELL'S HIGHWAY (131657—$2.50)*
☐ CIMARRON #12: CIMARRON AND THE WAR WOMEN (132521—$2.50)*
☐ CIMARRON #13: CIMARRON AND THE BOOTLEGGERS (134494—$2.50)*
☐ CIMARRON #14: CIMARRON ON THE HIGH PLAINS (134850—$2.50)*
☐ CIMARRON #15: CIMARRON AND THE PROPHET'S PEOPLE

(135733—$2.50)*
☐ CIMARRON #16: CIMARRON AND THE SCALP HUNTERS (136659—$2.75)*

*Prices slightly higher in Canada

Buy them at your local
bookstore or use coupon
on next page for ordering.

34   84
Ⓢ 150 172 121

SIGNET Double Westerns You'll Enjoy

(0451

- [ ] BLOOD JUSTICE and THE VALIANT BUGLES by Gordon D. Shireffs
  (133390—$3.50)
- [ ] LAST TRAIN FROM GUN HILL and THE BORDER GUIDON by Gordon D Shireffs.
  (126874—$2.95)
- [ ] BITTER SAGE and THE BUSHWHACKERS by Frank Gruber.
  (129202—$3.50)
- [ ] QUANTRELL'S RAIDERS and TOWN TAMER by Frank Gruber.
  (127765—$3.50)
- [ ] FIGHTING MAN and THE MARSHALL by Frank Gruber. (116011—$2.50)
- [ ] RIDE TO HELL and LONESOME RIVER by Frank Gruber.
  (123476—$2.95)
- [ ] COMANCH' and RIDE THE WILD TRAIL by Cliff Farrell.
  (115651—$2.50)
- [ ] RETURN OF THE LONG RIDERS and TERROR IN EAGLE BASIN by Cliff Farrell.
  (118391—$2.75)
- [ ] CROSS FIRE and THE RENEGADE by Cliff Farrell. (123891—$2.95)
- [ ] THE MAN FROM YESTERDAY and THE GUNFIGHTERS by John S. Daniel
  (115996—$2.50)
- [ ] TROUBLE IN TOMBSTONE and BRAND OF A MAN by Tom Hopkins and Thomas Thompson.
  (116003—$2.50)

*Prices slightly higher in Canada
